Hit the Wall

Rochelle Paige

Crystal,

Love you!

♥ Rochelle

(PS - where is my Nico?)

Edited by Mickey Reed at Imabookshark.com

Cover designed by Kari Ayasha at Covertocoverdesigns.com

This is a work of fiction. Names, characters, places and incidents are the product of the author's imagination or are used factiously, and any resemblance to any actual persons or living or dead, events or locals are entirely coincidental.

ISBN: 1497339510
ISBN-13: 978-1497339514

DEDICATION

Mom –

Thank you for pushing me to reach for my own dream. I couldn't have done it without you.

CONTENTS

PROLOGUE

JACKSON

I couldn't believe that I had to deal with this bullshit. It was bad enough that I'd had to watch Lex fall for Drake, but now I had to go talk to Sasha about the crap she'd pulled to fuck with their relationship. I could have just kept my mouth shut and not said anything to Drake about Lex's job. I could have just enjoyed the fuck out of punching him and then waited to see if they'd stay broken up. But no, I hadn't been able to stand knowing that she'd been hurting when I could do something to fix it.

I'd grown up with Lex in my life, always thinking of her as my other little sister. She and Aubrey were attached at the hip, and she spent almost as much time at our house as she did her dad's. Then she hit her teens and filled out. I couldn't help but notice her new tits, and she started to show up in my spank bank. It freaked me out the first time I thought of her while jacking off in the shower, but I figured it was normal and shrugged it off. She was dating Brad, and there were plenty of girls in high school for me to mess around with.

The night I caught Brad cheating on her changed everything. I held her in my arms as she fell apart, and I realized I wanted her for my own. It was the absolute worst fucking timing to figure out that I didn't love her like a sister. I just loved her.

She needed time to get over Brad and what he had done. She wasn't ready for a boyfriend, and I couldn't just play with her. My mom would kill me if I didn't treat Lex right. I knew that when we got together that would be it. So I enjoyed the girls in college while I waited. Tried new things and discovered I liked my sex hard and rough. I waited some more so I could get it out of my system before going to her. I put it off so long that Drake swooped in and stole her right out from underneath my nose.

I knew the second I saw them together that I had waited too long. He wanted her, and I couldn't blame him. She was hot. Lots of guys wanted her. But it was the way she looked at him that got to me. Her eyes lit up any time he was near, and she'd get this look on her face. Like he was the only thing she could see. I tried to tell myself that it was only a fling and that it was a good sign. She was ready for a relationship again. I just had to wait until Drake messed up before I could finally have Lex. But when it came down to it, I just couldn't do it. She loved him, and he made her happy. More than anything, I wanted her to be happy.

When Drake calmed down and listened to me, the look of horror on his face told me that he loved her, too. My worst fear was confirmed when he refused to budge from her dorm, unwilling to go anywhere until he could find Lex. By the time Aubrey finally answered her phone, I felt sorry for the guy. He was a total wreck from knowing how much he had hurt Lex. If she forgave him, he wasn't ever going to let her go. So I had to do it.

Now here I was, on my way to find Sasha to make sure she didn't interfere in their relationship again. Talk about an awkward conversation. I had to talk to a chick I'd banged the fuck out of last year. About not messing with the girl I was in love with and her boyfriend. The situation was so fucked up that I couldn't have made this shit up if I tried.

CHAPTER 1

KAYLIE

The shouting from next door woke me up, and I was not happy to have my much-needed rest interrupted. I'd worked late at the bar last night, covering a shift for one of the other bartenders. After a full day of classes and a tough practice for my upcoming show, the last thing I needed was to only get a few hours of sleep because Sasha had something going down yet again. That girl had more drama in her life than a daytime soap opera.

I waited a couple minutes to see if the subject of her latest tirade would storm out and let me catch a little more rest. No such luck. It seemed like their argument was escalating from what I could hear, so I hopped out of bed and stomped next door to bang on the door.

"What the fuck?!" I heard as the door was thrown open. My jaw dropped at the sight of Jackson Silver in Sasha's room. I hadn't thought he'd had it in him to care enough about any woman to get into a shouting match with her with the way he blew through all the girls on campus, except maybe his sister and her best friend. Not that I didn't totally get why so many girls went crazy over him, with his tousled blond hair, wicked blue eyes, and insanely hot body. But he was the epitome of love 'em and leave 'em, never spending more than a few nights with the same one.

"Ummmm…" I stuttered in response.

"You don't want to get in the middle of this, little girl," he growled at me.

I glanced at Sasha, who was standing behind him with tears streaking down her cheeks. She was usually so perfectly put together, but she looked a total wreck right now with her hair mussed up and mascara smudged everywhere. She wasn't my favorite person in the world, but it seemed like she could use a little bit of help right about now.

"No, I really don't want to get in the middle of whatever is going on here," I said as I waved my hand between the two of them, "but I'm exhausted and I really need some sleep. And Sasha looks like she's had enough. So why don't you head out and leave this for another time and place?"

"Hell no! This isn't the kind of shit that can wait. Once she convinces me she will stay out of things that are none of her business, I'll leave. Now run along like a good girl." He turned his head to glare at Sasha. "I'm sure we won't be much longer, will we, Sasha?"

"Jackson, please let me explain. You hurt me so much—" she cried, reaching out to grab his arm.

"Stop! You can't use that as an excuse. I did nothing to hurt you that you didn't ask me to do," he snapped back at her. I gasped and his gaze swiveled back to me. He ran his hands through his messy hair and looked down at the floor. "Fuck! Look, I swear that I will be out of here soon. I don't want to be here any more than you want to be awake right now."

"Well, then you won't mind if I wait while you wrap this up and leave," I replied, leaning against the doorway with my arms crossed.

Jackson's eyes trailed down to my chest, where my breasts—sans bra—were lifted up by my arms. A smirk curled the edge of his lips and he glanced back up at my face. "Really? You're going to take Sasha's back? No questions asked? Is that supposed to scare me into behaving or something, little girl? Because I'm a lot bigger than you are."

"Look, I don't know what's going on here, but I can't just leave when she's a mess and you're all intimidating and stuff. So just say what you've gotta say and let's get this over with, okay?"

His smirk turned into a full-fledged grin. "You wanna stay for this? Feel free," he said before turning back to Sasha. "I don't know what the fuck you were thinking, but the stunt you pulled with Drake's parents almost ruined his relationship with Lex."

"But—" Sasha interrupted.

Jackson waved her off. "I'm not done yet. You need to understand that, even if your plan had worked, you still wouldn't have ended up with him in your bed. He loves her. He wouldn't have just forgotten about her and moved on to you, especially when he realized you were the reason he lost Lex."

"That wasn't what I wanted," she protested.

'Then why the fuck did you try to break them up if you didn't want Drake for yourself? Was it just for shits and giggles?" Jackson asked. It was the question I had been thinking myself.

Sasha tried to defend her actions. "I don't know! I didn't even have a plan. I heard the rumor about her job, and I shared it with my mom. That's all I did."

Jackson threw his hands up in frustration. "That's *all*? You had to have known that your mom would call Drake's mom. They're best friends. What the hell were you hoping would happen?"

"I told you! I didn't think that far ahead! I was just pissed and I did something stupid, okay? I don't get what you both see in her. That's all," Sasha explained, reaching out to try to grab Jackson's arm.

Sasha's answer blew me away. And it looked like Jackson felt the same. "Both? What the fuck? That's what this was all about? You just wanted to hurt Lex because you think she's the reason I didn't want a relationship with you last year?"

And there it was. The elephant in the room. Clearly they'd had a fling of some kind and Sasha had wanted more when she should have known better since Jackson never did relationships. And it sounded like the rumor mill had had it right with the talk of Alexa being the reason behind his endless string of one-night stands.

Sasha looked up at him pleadingly. "It isn't fair that Alexa has your heart wrapped around her little finger and then a guy like Drake falls for her too. I've known him all my life. He's a good guy. She doesn't deserve to have both of you falling at her feet. Maybe I wanted to knock her off the pedestal you've put her on a little bit. So what? Are you really going to say that you wouldn't have jumped at the chance to make Alexa yours if things had fallen apart for them?"

"You really are a spoiled brat, Sasha. That's exactly why neither of us fell at your feet. Maybe instead of trying to ruin Lex's happiness, you should take a page from her book and actually give a damn about other people and not just yourself."

"I did give a damn about you, but you just used me and tossed me aside!"

"You can lie to yourself as much as you'd like about what happened between us, but you asked to be used. You practically begged me for it," he taunted her. "We didn't have a relationship, and I certainly didn't make you any promises back then. But I will make you one now that you better pay attention to. Don't fuck around with the people I care about or I will make sure you regret it. Do you understand?"

"But, Jackson, just listen to me," Sasha protested.

"There's nothing you have to say that I need to hear except that you understand and won't try to mess things up for Lex anymore," he growled back.

Sasha dropped down onto her bed and looked up at Jackson with a defeated expression on her face. "Why won't you let me explain? After what happened between us, you should at least let me have my say!"

If I hadn't felt awkward before, the direction their argument had taken certainly made me feel that way now. I wished I hadn't insisted on staying. Being tired was bad enough, but witnessing this was guaranteed to start my day on the wrong foot.

"Jesus, are you rewriting history in your head? I don't know what fantasies you've built up in your head, but the only thing that happened between us was sex. And if I had to stand around and listen to every chick I've ever banged, then I would never have time to get anything done."

"You can really stand here and tell me that our time together wasn't good?" Sasha asked, like a dog with a bone, unwilling to let go.

"Honestly? Yeah, I had fun with you that weekend. But that's all it was for me—a little bit of fun. I thought I was pretty clear with you that's all it was and all it would ever be. If you thought you were more than a quick lay to me, that's your own damn fault. So don't take it out on Lex."

"Arghhhhh!!" Sasha jumped up and stomped her foot in

frustration. "I am so sick and tired of hearing about Alexa!"

"Then let me make this easy for you. You stay away from Lex and Drake and you won't have to hear about her anymore. And if you don't, then I will just have to ruin the rest of the time you have left on campus. Don't doubt for a second that I won't do it, Sasha. Do you understand what I am saying to you?"

"Yes, fine. I'll leave your precious Alexa alone," she sneered.

"Then I'm done here," he said as he turned towards me. "Sorry about disrupting your sleep. It won't happen again since I should never have another reason to be here. But a bit of advice, you should choose your friends more wisely. Because Sasha sure as shit doesn't deserve someone taking her back like you just did."

"I never said we were friends, but even if we were, it wouldn't be any of your business," I said as I stepped out of the doorway so he could walk past. I shifted my gaze behind him to see Sasha watching both of us with a sour look on her face. "Now how about you head out so I can finally get back to sleep?"

"You're pretty sassy for such a little thing," he teased as he walked by.

"Jesus, Jackson. Seriously? You just totally wrecked me and now you're going to flirt with Kaylie right in front of me?" Sasha shrieked.

Jackson shook his head before he turned back to look at Sasha. "You have nobody to blame for this mess but yourself. And that wasn't flirting. You want to see me flirt?" he asked as he leveled his gaze at me and trailed his eyes down my body and back up again. He lifted his arms up to grip the doorframe, boxing me in as he leaned closer. "I'd be happy to show her what flirting looks like if you're game," he whispered against my ear, sending shivers up my spine.

"I think I'll pass. I've had enough excitement for the day already," I breathed out on a sigh.

"That's probably for the best. I guess I'll see you around. Kaylie, was it?"

I nodded my head in response. "Yes, Kaylie Rhodes."

He flashed me a smug grin before turning to walk away. I heard Sasha move behind me and didn't think anything of it until she shoved me through the doorway. "Thanks for nothing," she snapped at me. "A word of advice. Stay away from Jackson if you know what's good for you. He might use his body to give you the best night of sex you will ever have, but he won't offer anything beyond that."

"I'm not you, Sasha. I won't make the same mistakes you have."

"That's what you say now, but I saw the way you were looking at him. Just don't say I didn't warn you," she said before slamming the door in my face.

I wandered next door to my room, mulling over my encounter with Jackson. He definitely was hot as shit, but there was no way I should go there. It was pretty clear from what I'd overheard that he was into things that I had no interest in trying. Add in that he was only interested in short flings because he was in love with his sister's best friend and starting anything up with him would be way too complicated. But that shiver being near him had sent up my spine? That could mean trouble for me. I wasn't sure I would be able to resist him if he decided to make a play for me even though I knew I should.

I was just lying back down when Charlotte stormed into the room, two coffees and a bakery bag in her hand. She and I had been paired up as roommates our freshman year in what was probably the strangest match-up ever. She was from a huge family, and on the surface she seemed like the perfect Southern belle. Until you got to know Charlotte and realized that under the shiny surface was a wicked sense of humor that could rip you to shreds if you crossed her or someone she cared about. And I was lucky enough to be one of those people even though I wasn't used to developing truly close relationships.

After losing my parents and spending a couple years with my ice queen of an aunt, I'd learned to keep my distance from people. I'd put up walls to protect myself, but Charlotte had refused to stay at arm's length. She was always doing nice things and had been super patient with me. Before I'd known it, I'd found myself talking to her about the highs and lows of my day.

At five foot four, I wasn't exactly tall, but she was a tiny dynamo compared to me. Calling her a steel magnolia seemed so cliché, but she really did have a backbone that just wouldn't quit. And once she decided she liked you, there was no swaying her from her decision. There had been no way I was going to be able to change her mind, and soon, I hadn't wanted to anyway. She was an amazing person to have in your corner. Like today when she came bearing caffeine and treats to share while I was exhausted.

"Tada! Rise and shine, sugar," she chirped. "I bring you liquid gold to bribe you to join the land of the living."

"Gimme, gimme," I begged as I giggled.

"Gasp! What is my Kaylie-belle doing up this bright and early?" she teased, holding the cup of coffee just out of reach. "I usually have to drag your butt out of bed. Have you been holding out on me all this time? Waking up while I am out and about bright and early so you can get alone time and then feigning sleep when I get back?"

"Of course not! Whatever could possibly have woken me up from a deep sleep? I'll give you one guess with just a little clue. Her name rhymes with Tasha and she lives right next door."

"Shut up!" Charlotte said, handing me one of the cups. "What did I miss?"

"You are not going to believe this, but she and Jackson Silver were in the middle of a shouting match about Sasha trying to break up Drake and Alexa," I said before taking a big gulp of my coffee.

"For real? Did ya eavesdrop shamelessly?" she asked "Please, please, please make my day and say that you did. I'd love to have been a fly on the wall for that one. Ooooh, I bet that Jackson put Sasha in her place super fast. He's always struck me as the kind of guy who wouldn't take crap from anyone. C'mon now. Spill!"

"Gee, I don't know. Are you sure you're really interested? 'Cause I couldn't really tell, gossip girl," I teased while I reached for the bag to peek inside, but Charlotte held it just out of reach.

"Ah, ah, ah. Sharing is a two-way street. You know, I was fixin' to share these yummy cranberry muffins with you since they're your favorite, but if you can't be bothered to spill the sordid details from this morning's escapade, then I just might have to eat them all myself."

"Like I wasn't going to tell you anyway. No need to bribe me, but seriously. Hand them over or else. If I'm not going to get a good night's sleep, then at least I can start my day out right," I answered with my hand held out for the bag, which was a good thing because she tossed it at my head. I managed to grab it before the muffins spilled out and pulled one out to munch on as I continued. "Thanks for these. They will make the day almost bearable."

"Ummm, hello? I don't want your gratitude. I want my story, and I want it now! That boy's so bad he whups his own ass twice a week. I bet Sasha would have been shakin' in her boots if she had any."

"I know she's not your favorite person, Char, but Jackson was royally pissed at her. He is not the kind of guy I would want to cross, and she wasn't making things any better for herself. Although he was cool about me insisting that I wasn't going to leave them alone until he was ready to leave."

"Whoa there. Hold up a second. Are you telling me you went next door to interrupt their argument?" Charlotte asked.

"I know, I know, but I had to do it. I just went over expecting to ask them to keep it down, but then Jackson made a joke about me being a little girl, and what was I supposed to do then? He irritated me, and Sasha looked like she could use some support. So I stayed, but believe me when I say that I wish I hadn't."

"Why? What happened?" Charlotte asked as she plopped down onto her bed across from me.

"Nothing much, really. He yelled at her. She whined. He tried to make sure she wouldn't hurt Alexa again. She blamed it all on him, his screwing her over after they had sex and the fact that he's really in love with Alexa. Then he made it very clear that she pretty much was just an easy lay for him, and Sasha argued that it must have meant something to him. When she finally got the message, Sasha agreed to leave them alone. Jackson flirted with me a bit as he was leaving, and then she was a bitch to me and warned me away from him before slamming the door on me on my way out," I blurted out as quickly as possible while hoping that Charlotte wouldn't pounce on the bit about Jackson flirting with me.

"What?" she shrieked. "You went over there to help her out and Sasha had the nerve to slam the door on you? I swear she's one fry short of a Happy Meal, that girl. And you wonder why I don't like her that much. Well there you go. She's an ungrateful bitch. It would totally serve her right if you started dating Jackson and she was forced to see the two of you together living next door to us and all."

"Yeah, she's an ungrateful bitch, but you can be a vengeful one so I'm glad you're on my side and not hers," I teased as Charlotte rubbed her hands together like she was plotting something. Usually when that happened, it didn't bode well for someone else.

"So when you said that Jackson flirted with you, what did he say? Did he seem interested, or was it 'let me get in your panties' for a bit type of flirting?"

"Char, stop! I am so not going to go there. It's pointless because you and I both know he doesn't do relationships. And as sexy as he might be, he just isn't my type," I protested.

"Oh, please. Jackson Silver is every girl's type. That's why he's been able to go through so many girls on campus. Can you honestly sit there and tell me that he doesn't make your panties the teeniest bit wet?"

I held my hand up to interrupt her flow of thought before she got going any further. "Jesus, Char! Fine, yes, I will admit he's hot. But he's super intense, doesn't do anything but super-quick hook-ups, and based on what I overheard between him and Sasha, I don't think we would be a good match in bed."

"It's not like your relationships last that long anyway. And you always pick safe guys so you don't risk getting hurt too much. Maybe you need to go out with someone more like Jackson, even if it's not him. A guy who will challenge you a little bit, who won't let you dictate the pace of your relationship.

One who won't let you get away with keeping him at arm's length," Charlotte said before hopping out of her bed and climbing into mine with me. "I worry about you. We're graduating soon, and I won't be there to make sure that you pick well if you wait to really fall for someone once we're gone."

I wrapped my arms around her as I realized that she was really worried about me. "I love you too, Char. No matter how far apart from each other we end up, I promise that you will get the chance to give me the thumbs up or down on guys, okay? But I really worry about your choices if you think that Jackson would be considered picking well. You don't even know anything about him except that he's hot and intense."

She looked at me, her green eyes narrowed on mine as she replied. "I know more than that, Kaylie. He's someone who managed to get a rise out of you, you think he's hot even if you won't admit it, and it would piss Sasha off. I get that the third reason isn't a good one, but the first two work for me. Add in that his sister is pretty awesome from what you've said about her when you talked about helping Aubrey out in the dance class you're taking together and he can't be all that bad."

"Except that he's a man-whore!" I protested.

"And my mama always said that reformed rakes make the best husbands. Hell, look at Shane. He was a huge player in high school before he met me our senior year, and he settled right down and into a long-distance relationship when I decided to come here for school. He'd like nothing more than to put his ring on my finger, and nobody would have ever expected it of him four years ago," Charlotte argued.

I stopped to consider the point she was making, and it was a good one. Just because a guy played around a lot didn't mean that when he really fell for a girl he wouldn't be able to be faithful. If anything, maybe at our age it would make him more likely to be able to not cheat since he'd already been with so many other women and worked it out of his system. But that didn't mean that Jackson Silver was the guy for me, and I wasn't even looking for Mr. Right in my life. Maybe a Mr. Right Now, but not a forever guy. Charlotte was relentless when she was trying to make a point though. Better to deflect the conversation now or spend the rest of the semester with her trying to catch Jackson for me.

"I hear what you're saying, and if I meet a guy like that who's totally into me, I promise to at least consider giving him a chance. But I am really glad you mentioned Shane and a ring. Do you think he's going to pop the question over Christmas break? Because as you pointed out to me, we are graduating soon, and I'm sure he's hoping that you'll be ready to come back home and become Mrs. Shane Sorenson."

She flopped down onto my pillows and tossed her right arm over her face, covering her eyes. "Ugh! I just don't know. I love Shane, I really do. But do I really want to take my brand-new college degree back to the middle of nowhere in Tennessee and hope that my parents will use some of my ideas to market the bar while Shane's training horses at his dad's place?"

"You know your parents will listen to your ideas. They might not use them all, but they pushed for you to go away to college so you could spread your wings a bit," I reminded her.

"I know," she sighed. "I guess I just pictured something different for my future than the same life in a small town that my parents have."

"Then tell Shane that. Give him a chance to give you the something different that you're dreaming of. He worships the ground you walk on. Are you ready to walk away and give him up?"

"No! I can't picture my life without him in it," she protested. "We didn't survive four years of college and a long-distance relationship only for me to dump him when I graduate. I just need to figure out what I want. But I hate the thought of him making any more sacrifices to be with me."

"You both made sacrifices to be together," I reminded her. "You've missed out on lots of things here because you have a boyfriend waiting at home for you. Don't forget that. Plus, he's the one who pushed for you guys to stay together when you left."

"You're right. I just wish I was happier about going home is all," Charlotte worried. "I really am looking forward to being closer to Shane. I'm just not excited about going back to small-town life."

"I hate to be the bearer of bad news, but it's not like you're living life in the fast lane up here, Char. Things can't be that much different on campus than they are back home. You've got the same gossip mill, and the campus is about the size of your town."

"True. I guess it's just that I dreamed of getting out, and now I'm going back right away. It's hard to explain."

As much as I loved Char, it was kind of hard to hear her complain about an option I would kill to have. "I hear what you're saying, but just remember how lucky you are to have a home, parents who will support any decision you make, and great guy to go back to when you graduate. I have no idea what I'm going to do or where I'm going to go. It's not like moving back in with my aunt is even an option since I'm an adult now."

"Oh, Kaylie. I'm such a whiny bitch! Ignore me. I'll figure out what I want soon enough, and you know that you are always welcome back home with me, too. My parents would love to have you while you're trying to decide between all the offers you know you're going to get! They can't wait to see you during break."

I chuckled in response to her enthusiasm. She wasn't exaggerating either. Her parents would absolutely let me stay with them while I was trying to decide what to do next. Although I doubted she was right about me getting offers to dance professionally. My decision to attend college at my parents' alma mater might come back to bite me in the ass when it came to that. But it had been worth it to spend four years feeling closer than ever to them.

CHAPTER 2

JACKSON

I'd never been happier for Christmas break in my life. Going to college in my hometown meant I could always do a quick laundry run or grab a home-cooked meal at my house. It also meant that breaks didn't seem so special since it was just a short drive home, but this time was different. I needed some space to come to terms with what I'd lost. Hell, what I had basically thrown away due to my own damn stupidity if I was being completely honest with myself.

I'd always assumed that there would be plenty of time for Lex and me to become a couple. It never fucking crossed my mind that she'd find someone else before I'd realized she was ready for a relationship again. She'd spent two years commuting to and from class while living at home with her dad, barely hitting the school's social scene unless Aubrey had dragged her to something.

So what had I done with that time while she had been healing? I'm a guy—I'd enjoyed myself while she hadn't been around. She wasn't my girlfriend yet, so I'd figured I would sow my wild oats before I tied myself to Lex. And I'd had a lot of oats to sow. I'd enjoyed myself, playing the field and pretty much trying anything and everything. It never ceased to amaze me what girls were willing to do to grab a guy's attention. I wanted to get it out of my system so that I could be a good husband and father like my dad. I'd worked damn hard at it too, blowing my way through a lot of chicks on campus while waiting for Lex to come around.

Then Lex's dad convinced her that she needed to get the full college experience, and she moved into the dorm with my sister. I knew it was the first step and made sure I stopped messing around because I didn't want my escapades to blow back on her. And I sure as hell didn't want Lex to think I was with some other girl when she was ready to date again.

I thought that I had it all planned out. I knew that my sister would make it easy for me, and I was right. When she asked me if they could come to the first frat party of the school year, I jumped at the chance to hang out with Lex. I knew she wouldn't be very excited about a frat party, so I decided to steal her away to my room to watch movies, letting her think that I was rescuing her when I really just wanted her all to myself before my frat brothers got too close of a look at her.

I guess I wasn't fast enough since Drake saw her when we went to grab one last beer before heading upstairs. Even in the middle of his argument with Sasha, I knew he had noticed her, and I made sure he thought she was mine already. And I sure as shit didn't introduce the two of them after I'd seen her checking him out. I let Lex think whatever she wanted when she wondered why I hadn't introduced them to each other, half hoping she'd assume he was a douche and stay away from him. What I hadn't counted on was Drake's booking a flight with her dad and her going along as co-pilot. Or his deciding to chase after her hard once he'd realized that she wasn't my girl. And certainly not her falling for him so hard and fast that the next time I saw her she was already out of my reach.

I wanted to blame Drake, but it was my own damn fault that I hadn't moved faster. I'd wasted time on girls whose names I didn't even remember the next morning instead of making it clear to Lex that I wanted her for my own. I wanted to be pissed at Lex for falling for Drake, but how could I when she was so disgustingly happy? She looked at him in a way that she never had me, and I needed to deal with the fact that she'd only ever seen me as her big brother. And that was what this break was going to be all about for me—taking time to adjust to a future without her in it as anything other than my friend and unofficial part of the family.

I pulled my truck into the driveway and was happy to see that I'd beat Aubrey home. She was bummed that Lex wasn't going to be around much this break and didn't understand why I wasn't pissed that our holiday traditions were going to change now that Lex was going to be out of town with Drake's family. I figured that she knew something was up with how I'd looked at Lex and how I'd reacted to her and Drake, but she sure as shit wasn't going to bring it up to me. And there was no way in hell I was going to talk to my little sister about this. She would freak out at the idea that she could have had Lex as her sister-in-law. Then she'd be totally bummed that it wasn't going to happen before finally swinging back to being thrilled that Lex was so happy with Drake.

I walked into the house, happy to have a little bit of time to myself, but then I saw my dad waiting inside. I knew he was going to have questions about how I felt about Lex and Drake, but I wasn't sure that I was ready to answer them. I loved my dad. Don't get me wrong. But I hadn't come to terms with how I was gonna handle everything later. I wasn't ready to answer questions yet.

My dad walked up to me and pulled me into a big bear hug. I allowed myself a moment to just enjoy my dad's closeness before I backed away to look him in the eyes.

"Hey, Dad," I said as he smiled at me. I could see the concern in his expression.

"Jackson?" he asked cautiously. "You doing okay?"

I looked down at the floor, not ready for him to see all of my feelings I'm sure were showing on my face. Most people couldn't read my emotions very easily, but my dad nailed it every single time. "Yeah, Dad. I'm fine," I answered. There was a pause, and my dad didn't say anything, so I glanced back up at him. I just needed some time to wrap my head around the fact that Lex was gone.

"It'll be okay. I promise, son. You know that I love Lex like my own daughter, and your mom and I would've been thrilled to have her as a daughter-in-law. We saw the way you started to look at her after everything fell apart with Brad, and I'll admit that we would have loved it if you guys became a couple. That being said, I need to be blunt because I think you need to hear this."

"Dad," I interrupted, "I'm not really ready to talk about it yet."

"I don't want you to say anything. I just want you to listen and think about this while you're working it all out in your head. I know you feel like you love her, and you probably do. But I'm just not sure that it's the type of love you think it is."

"You don't know that!"

"Jackson, you aren't the most patient person in the world. You know that. And yet you waited two years for Lex to come around to the idea of dating again. If your feelings really ran deep, I don't know that you could have waited that long without doing anything about it. I'm sorry if what I am saying sounds harsh, but you need to think about whether or not your guilt over everything that happened just made you see her in a different light or if you really wanted her that way. Because, son, believe me when I say that when you meet the right one, you will know beyond a shadow of a doubt. And I don't think you're the type of guy who would spend a couple years messing around with other girls when she's right there in front of you."

I got the point my dad was trying to make, but right now he was just pissing me off. "Just stop right there, Dad. I'm not going to let you discount what I feel for Lex and what it means that she's with Drake now."

"That's not what I am trying to do here, son. Maybe it's too early for you. I get that you need time to figure this out on your own. Just promise me that you'll think about what I've said while you're doing that, okay?"

"Sure, Dad. Whatever," I said, barely able to stop myself from rolling my eyes at him.

"So, awkward change of subject here, but I figured you might need to blow off some steam so I called the dojo to see if they needed any help. Sensei would appreciate it if you can help teach a few classes this week."

"Great. I think I'll just grab my stuff and head over there then. I'm sure there's plenty of stuff I can do to help out if there isn't a class going right away," I said before heading upstairs to grab my karate bag.

I might not have been happy to hear what my dad had had to say, but he had really helped me out by setting things up for me to hang out at the dojo. It had always been the place I went to clear my mind. A lot of people didn't get how fighting brought me peace. But karate wasn't about the fighting to me as much as it was about self-control, focus, and discipline. And I could really use that focus right about now.

I knew it was going to be a rough couple weeks, but I hadn't expected to be blindsided this early by that conversation with my dad. I'd hoped that he had already talked to my mom and we could all just enjoy this break without everyone asking me a bunch of questions about my feelings and shit. My time at the dojo was just what I needed to center me.

I spent a few hours teaching classes and loved the look on the faces of the kids when I would show them a new move. It reminded me of when my dad started bringing me to class when I was little. It was crazy to think that now the kids watched me and hoped they would one day be able to do the same moves.

After the class, I had the dojo all to myself and was able to run through some katas before I headed back home. As I began each kata, I took a single deep breath to clear out my mind and calm my nerves. Sensei had taught me that the kata should be regarded as a moving meditation of sorts. I envisioned that my imaginary opponents were real and used enough force so that every strike within the form could be a finishing one. By the time I was done, I was sweating bullets and breathing heavily.

When I got back home and pulled into the driveway, I parked my truck behind Aubrey's car, ready for a quick escape if I needed it. As I walked into the house, I could hear my sister in the kitchen with Mom. It smelled like dinner was almost ready, but I needed to squeeze a shower in before joining everyone, so I headed straight upstairs before saying hello. I'd never make it out of the kitchen in time with both of them in there.

I tossed my bag into the laundry room, figuring that my mom would clean up my gi if I left it there for her. Strolling into my bathroom, I blasted the water as hot as I could make it before stripping out of my clothes and jumping into the steam. Leaning my head under the water, I just stood there for a moment, enjoying the heat that wrapped around me.

Images of Lex over the last couple of years played through my mind, and I couldn't help but wonder if my dad was right. Had I been able to wait so patiently because I'd been wrong about what I'd been feeling? It wasn't like when I had been banging those other chicks that I'd been thinking about her either. Could I have been totally wrong all this time? Was that why it had been so easy for me to help Drake realize how badly he'd fucked up when they got into their fight? I hadn't even thought twice about setting him straight about her. If I'd really wanted her for myself, wouldn't it have at least crossed my mind to not say a word and watch their relationship implode?

I shook my head, trying to get the images and questions out of my head. The last thing I needed before heading back down for dinner was to seem like I was worried about something. My mom would see it and act like a shark smelling blood in the water. It was time to paste on a happy face and fake it so she wouldn't know how much this was on my mind. That little talk with my dad had already been bad enough. I definitely wanted to avoid having a similar one with my mom.

Everyone was getting ready to sit down to dinner by the time I made it back downstairs. It was only the four of us since both of my older brothers were celebrating the holidays with their wives' families. All of my favorites were on the table, a sure sign that my mom already knew something was up. She'd always used food for comfort. It was a goddamn miracle that neither Aubrey nor I had been fat growing up. I guess it was a lucky thing that our dad had kept us busy enough to work off all the calories our mom had given us.

I pulled out my mom's chair, helping her get settled. "Hey, Mom," I said as I leaned down to kiss her cheek.

"Hi, baby boy," she smiled up at me. "So happy to have you home for break."

Yes, my mom was big on nicknames and still liked to call me her baby. It didn't matter how often I tried to remind her that I was bigger than her. She'd just remind me that she'd carried me for nine months and would always remember me as small as I was when I was born with a sappy-as-shit look on her face. So I didn't bother saying anything anymore and let it pass, shaking my head as I walked over to my chair.

Aubrey was practically bouncing in her seat with excitement. "Only four more days until Christmas! I can't wait to make cookies and go shopping and see what amazing presents you got me this year!"

My dad chuckled at her enthusiasm. "Presents? I don't remember buying any gifts for you this year. Are you sure you weren't on the naughty list this year?" he teased.

"Oh, please, Daddy. Like Mom would let you do the shopping. You just haven't seen the credit card bills yet, but I am sure she picked me out something fabulous like she always does. But don't worry. You'll still get lots of hugs and kisses from me as a thank-you."

And that was my sister, buttering up our dad and laying the groundwork for extra gifts. How could he not run out and pick up something for her himself after that comment? She had him wrapped around her little finger and knew how to work him almost as well as our mom did.

I listened to their conversation flow around me, tossing in a comment here and there while watching the clock, ready for dinner to be over. I felt my mom and dad's concerned glances several times through the night. Aubrey chattered on, drawing their attention away each time. I knew my sister was a talker, but this was a bit much even for her. Which confirmed the fact that they all knew about my feelings for Lex and were worried. So much for a quiet break where I could get my head screwed back on right without anyone asking questions. Fuck!

CHAPTER 3

KAYLIE

I loved bartending at the campus bar, The Rooster's Nest. Of course, nobody called it by the real name. Instead, everyone usually just called it The Roost. Or if they were feeling particularly pervy, they called it The Cock. The bar was known for its cold beers, its hot cheese fries, and college bands. It's a bit of a dive, but not in a sleazy way. Although the tight t-shirts we wore with crazy phrases like "I Serve Tail at The Cock" and a picture of a martini glass on it sure did seem push things toward the sleazy slide.

I got the job as soon as I'd turned twenty-one. I needed the money, and it paid well for a part-time job with hours that didn't interfere with school or dance. It also didn't hurt that I usually got to work shifts with my roomie Charlotte since she was the one who'd gotten me the interview. She was the boss's favorite at The Roost, so I'd been a shoe-in for the job. And I got paid well to flirt all night, so that was a plus too.

Speaking of hot guys, Jackson Silver walked into the bar about an hour before last call. I'd thought about him several times over the last month and a half. Word on campus was that he'd been keeping to himself a lot more. When he came back from Christmas break, there hadn't been any more rumors about random hook-ups. This was the first time I'd seen him since witnessing his argument with Sasha, which was strange considering how small the campus was.

He sat down at the other side of the bar, so Charlotte took

his order and served him a beer and a shot. Then she headed straight over to me as soon as she had taken care of Jackson.

"Did ya see who's at the bar? Hottie McHot-Pants himself," she said, nodding her head in his direction.

"Yeah, I saw him." I replied.

She snorted in response. "Like I didn't know that already. I could practically feel you staring through my shoulder blades while I was servin' him. Damn, girl. Something ya forgot to tell me about you and Jackson? Did y'all bump uglies or something after his fight with Sasha?" she teased. "C'mon. Make Momma proud. Tell me you had a wild 'n' crazy time and let him do all sorts of nasty things to you. Or at the very least that you've been thinking about what I said and are finally open to the idea of dating someone like him. Or maybe him for real."

I whipped her ass with my towel and didn't bother responding. Charlotte knew that I wasn't into one-night stands, and that was all Jackson used to do, maybe extending them to a weekend if the mood struck him. I didn't bother with the whole love thing, but if I was going to let a guy get that close to me, then I had to at least know and like him.

There was no doubt that Jackson was super hot, but I wasn't sure that he was very likable, so there wasn't any use going there. So of course I hadn't thought about going out with him. That much. Except after watching Charlotte with Shane over break, I couldn't get her comments about reformed players making the best boyfriends out of my head, and I wanted to kill her for it now.

I glanced over at him one more time before refocusing on my own customers.

The time to close flew by, and the next thing I knew, Charlotte was racing over to me as the bar started to empty out. I figured she was going to beg me to handle cleanup so that she could head back to the dorm to have some private webcam time with her boyfriend back home before I made it back.

"Shit, Kaylie. I fucked up," she whispered to me as she grabbed my arm.

"What's wrong?" I asked. It wasn't like Charlotte to freak out about anything. She was usually so laid back.

"I didn't realize Jackson had been drinking before he got here. He seemed fine, and now he's totally trashed. I swear to God I had no idea I was over-serving him. I only gave him a couple beers and one shot, but now he's totally smashed and I can't let him drive back to campus. I'm screwed. If something happens to him, I am so fucked," she lamented.

I glanced down the bar to see Jackson hunched over with his head resting on his arms, eyes closed. Char hadn't been exaggerating when she said she was screwed, even if she was the bar's star employee. She couldn't let him drive if he'd had too much to drink, and our boss would not like the idea of the town's golden boy going home in a cab from his bar. There was no way that was going to work as a solution to this mess.

"How about this? I'll just drive Jackson back in his car and you take mine."

"Are you sure that's a good idea, Kaylie? I know I've been teasing you about dating him, but you don't know him that well, and the rumors on campus about his tastes don't really inspire confidence. Especially when he's trashed. I'm not sure I feel comfortable with you cleaning up my mess by leaving with him even in his condition," Charlotte worried aloud.

"It'll be fine, Charlotte. He just needs a ride. Besides, if he didn't hurt Sasha after the stunt she pulled, then he isn't going to do anything to me just because I am helping him out with a ride home. Don't be such a worrywart. I'll even text his sister to let her know what's going on so she can check on him in the morning, okay?"

"I don't know about this, Kaylie. It doesn't feel right that you're taking care of this for me. I should just take him."

I hugged her to me. 'First of all, you're my best friend. Of course I'm going to help you whenever I can. Secondly, he's Aubrey's brother, so I wouldn't feel right leaving him like this even if this had happened somewhere else where we were just drinking and not serving. More importantly, it's not like you can be the one to drive him back yourself. Shane would flip the fuck out if you told him you were alone in a car with a drunk hot guy even though it was perfectly innocent," I reminded her.

"Why don't we just text Aubrey now and ask her to come get him?" she asked.

"Because it's already one o'clock in the morning. I'm not going to drag her out of bed when I'm already here. Relax. It's not a big deal. Besides, you get to make it up to me by being on clean-up duty tonight," I replied, tossing my towel at her before rounding the bar to walk over to Jackson.

"Hey, buddy, let's get you home. You don't look so good," I said before I helped Jackson to his feet. He looked up at me with glazed eyes and I noticed his flushed cheeks. I reached out and rested my hand on his forehead, realizing that he wasn't drunk. He was sick. "Damn, you picked a bad time to come out to the bar. Didn't you realize that you were coming down with something?"

Jackson shook his head, but I wasn't sure if it was in response to my question or to try to wake up a little. "No, I'm fine. I never get sick."

"Sure you don't. How about I shoot your sister a text and then help you get home safely?" I asked. I held my palm out to him as I continued. "Now where are your car keys?"

"I said I'm fine. There's no way I'm going to let a little girl like you drive my truck," he rasped back at me.

"Okie-dokie then. Wow, you sure do like to remind me that you're bigger than me. How about I walk you out and make sure you make it to your big manly truck, okay?" I teased as I watched him stagger on his way to the door. He really was in no condition to drive. Hopefully he'd realize it before I had to fight him for his keys, because as much as it irritated me when he called me little, he was still much bigger than I was.

I shot Aubrey a quick text to let her know that her brother was sick while I trailed behind him. I figured she was probably asleep, but at least she'd know to check on him in the morning to make sure he was all right. We had just made it outside when I got a response back from her asking me if I'd be willing to take him to their parents' house. Apparently he's a big baby when he's sick, so she thought it would be better for him if he wasn't at the frat house while he wasn't feeling well. She was going to let their mom know that we were on the way, and she was sure their dad would be able to drive me back to campus after.

By the time we made it to his truck, Jackson looked like he was about to pass out. I watched as he pulled his keys out of his front pocket, both glad and a little disappointed that I didn't have to fish for them myself. He fumbled with them while trying to unlock his car and they fell from his hand to the ground.

"Fuck," he mumbled under his breath.

"C'mon. I told your sister that I'd make sure you made it to your parents' house safe and sound so your mom can nurse you back to health." I reached down to snag his keys before he could grab them. "I promise to be extra careful with your precious truck if you'll just cooperate and get in."

He tried to level me with a glare, but it just didn't have any heat to it. "Shit, I think you're right. I feel like crap."

I tugged on his arm, walking him around to the passenger side. "C'mon then. Get in. I'll have you to your parent's house in no time flat," I said as I opened the door and half-pushed him inside. He didn't even fight. He just climbed into the car and leaned back with his eyes closed.

When I got into the driver's seat, I had to pull it all the way forward and up so I could see over the dash. I turned the key in the ignition and breathed a deep sigh of relief that it was an automatic and not manual. I glanced across at Jackson and realized that he'd fallen fast asleep sometime during the time it took me to get situated. I sent Charlotte a quick text to tell her about the change in plans, plugged the address into my phone's GPS, and pulled out of the parking lot.

It was a quick drive to his parents' and we were there before I knew it. Which was a good thing because my hormones were going crazy with his scent floating in the air. As much as I didn't like the idea of wanting him, my body was making it clear that it disagreed with me. It didn't help that I was seeing him at a vulnerable point right now either. I needed to get him out of the truck and into the house and then get myself out of here fast. As I climbed out, the porch lights turned on and his mom opened the front door. She came rushing out to help me get Jackson inside.

"Hi, I'm Megan, Jackson's mom. Thanks so much for bringing him home to me," she said as she reached us. "Aubrey said you're Kaylie, right?"

"Yup, that's me."

"It was awfully sweet of you to do this for him. We're so lucky you were there and realized he was in trouble. I don't know what I would do if anything happened to my baby boy," she continued as she led him into the house with me following behind, giggling a little. "I know. He hates when I call him that, but I just can't help myself since he's my youngest boy. Especially when he's sick and I get to mother him."

"I'll have to keep that in mind the next time I see him on campus. I'm sure he'll like it even less if I call him that since he likes to call me little girl."

"Yes! Definitely tease him about it if he calls you that. I didn't realize you knew each other. I thought you were a friend of Aubrey's?" she asked.

I closed the door behind us before answering. "I don't really know Jackson that much. We've just seen each other around a few times."

"Well, thank you so much for stepping in and helping him out after he's irritated you those few times. I really appreciate it." She waved me towards the living room couch. "Why don't you wait down here while I get him settled upstairs? His dad is running late from a business dinner a few towns over, but he should be back soon to give you a lift back to campus."

I sat down and waited, glancing around the room and looking at all the family photos displayed on the walls. Ones of Jackson and Aubrey and their two older brothers at all stages of life, from baby to their high school graduations. Jackson was an adorable baby, but he looked a little awkward in his early teens. There were several of him looking sexy in some sort of martial arts gear closer to his age now. It was weird getting a peek into his life like this. Everything seemed so different than what I would have imagined from how he was on campus.

I tapped a text out to Char so that she knew I had made it here safely and to let her know that I was waiting for Jackson's dad to give me a ride home. Soon, my eyes started drifting shut since I was tired from a long day. Friday nights at the bar always wore me out since they capped off a full day of classes and kicked off the weekend for everyone else.

I felt someone nudge my shoulder, and I blearily opened my eyes. "Hey, sweetie. Why don't you just crash in Aubrey's room for the night? She won't mind, and I changed the sheets in there this week," Jackson's mom said.

I was exhausted and could barely keep my eyes open. It was probably a good idea, so I simply nodded and followed her upstairs. I pulled my clothes off and threw on the oversized shirt she'd brought for me to sleep in. Crawling under the sheets, I pretty much passed out right away.

When I woke up the next morning, I found a ton of messages from Char, who was pissed because I hadn't made it back last night and had slept through her checking up on me. Her last one said that I'd better be okay or she was going to kick Jackson's ass. I sent her a quick text letting her know I had just slept over instead of waiting up for Jackson's dad and that I'd be back soon.

I stumbled out of Aubrey's room to look for a bathroom, feeling icky because I hadn't washed up or brushed my teeth before I fell asleep. I barely made it five steps into the hallway before a door was flung open and Jackson stepped out wearing nothing but his underwear. His hair was all mussed from sleep and his eyes had a tired sleepy look to them right before they opened wide upon seeing me.

"Fuck!" he swore before grabbing my arm and pulling me into his room. "I cannot believe that I brought a chick home to my parents' house last night. What the hell was I thinking? Shit. My dad is going to fucking kill me."

I couldn't help the giggle that escaped when I realized he had the totally wrong idea. "Jackson," I started, attempting to interrupt him to let him know what had happened.

"Sorry, babe, but I need to get you out of here before anyone knows you were here. I'm sure last night was fun, but I never bring girls back here. Ever. I don't know what the hell happened last night or how much we had to drink. I had to have been out of my mind to do this though," he continued as he searched the room for my clothes. "Look, I know this sounds harsh, but I can't even remember your name."

"Jackson, stop. You've got it all wrong—" I tried again, but he ignored me a second time as he ran his hands through his hair and rubbed his eyes.

"Yeah, I know what you're going to say. Last night meant more than I realized and you want to see me again," he said before looking at my bare legs, which were peeking out of the bottom of the shirt his mom had given me. "And maybe we can do this again at my frat house or your place. It must've been good for me to let you sleep in one of my favorite shirts," he continued as he reached a finger out to lift the bottom of the shirt up.

"Listen, you don't I understand," I argued as I pushed his hand away and grabbed the doorknob to get out of there.

"Jackson," we both heard his mom say from the other side of the door. "Are you feeling any better?" she asked right before the door swung open, knocking me into Jackson's arms.

"Shit!" he swore as he caught me.

"Well, I guess that answers my question about you feeling better. If you're up to bothering Kaylie already, then you must not have come down with anything serious last night," she carried on as though she hadn't heard Jackson swear. "Kaylie, dear, I washed your clothes so you'd have something clean to change into this morning. Everything's waiting in the bathroom for you."

"Wait, what?" I heard Jackson say as I escaped his bedroom as quickly as I could, mortified that he'd seen me looking like this and worried that his mom might get the wrong idea after seeing me in there with nothing on but his shirt.

And it wasn't like it had even been my fault. He'd dragged me in there and wouldn't listen to a word I'd said. Geesh, how many one-night stands did a guy have had in order to assume that the girl he saw in his parents' hallway was some random chick he'd brought home with him? I got that I was dressed in his shirt and he didn't remember most of last night because he had been sick. But come on. That was one hell of an assumption to make.

I showered as fast as possible and was happy to be back in my own clothes. Hopefully his dad was up and ready to take me back to campus because I really didn't want to face Jackson again after what had just happened. I slowly pulled the door open and peeked in the hall, relieved to see that his door was closed. Rushing downstairs, I headed for what I assumed was the kitchen based on the noise I could hear from there.

As I rounded the corner, I bumped straight into what felt like a very warm brick wall. I glanced up and straight into laughing blue eyes. I swear to God, I had the worst luck possible with this guy.

"Hey," I greeted Jackson as I backed away.

"We've got to stop running into each other like this," he answered. "You in your pajamas at Sasha's door. Me almost ready to pass out at the bar. You in my favorite shirt outside my door. Me waiting to apologize to you for acting like an ass this morning."

"Wow. When you put it that way, it sounds really bad,

doesn't it? How about we just skip past all that and your dad can give me a lift back to my dorm?"

"No can do. My parents would be pissed if I let you run off without breakfast," he said, waving me toward the kitchen table, where scrambled eggs, bacon, and toast were already waiting. "Besides which, my dad has already left for the bank. So you're stuck with me for a ride home. My mom will be down in a second, but she has an appointment she needs to get to."

I sat down at the table, stumped by how I would get out of this. I was a nervous eater, so I filled my plate up as I snuck glances at Jackson.

"You don't have to look so thrilled at the idea of me giving you a ride home," he complainedas he piled eggs and toast on his own plate.

"Maybe I'm still waiting for that apology that you mentioned earlier. The one you owe me for being an ass when you assumed I was some booty call that you had to sneak out of your parents' house before anyone saw me?" I whispered since I could hear his mom coming down the stairs and didn't want to embarrass myself any further with her.

"I'm so glad to see you both eating," his mom said as she walked into the kitchen. "Jackson, you look none the worse for wear after feeling so ill last night. It's a good thing that your immune system is so disgustingly strong or you'd be down for days with the bug that's going around."

"It didn't seem so good last night with the way I felt," he complained.

"Well then it's a good thing Kaylie was there to rescue you, isn't it?" she reminded him before turning to me. "Thanks again for bringing him home last night. I'm sure it wasn't easy talking him into letting you help, especially since it meant you drove that beastly truck of his."

"I think he was just sick enough to listen to reason without putting up too much of a fight," I said.

"That's good to hear. I hope you don't mind that we've asked Jackson to give you a ride back to your dorm. My husband had an early morning meeting, and I need to run or I'm going to be late. And since he's apparently going to be heading in the same direction, it seemed to be the perfect solution."

"That will be fine, Mrs. Silver," I said. "Thanks for making me breakfast. I don't get to have a home-cooked meal like this very often."

"Oh, please call me Megan. You just saved my Jackson from what could have been a disastrous night and are friends with Aubrey from what she told me when she let me know you were on your way over. And you're more than welcome to come over any time you want a nice meal, sweetie."

"My mom really should have had more kids with the way she keeps trying to adopt all of the ones we bring home," Jackson joked.

"That's a good thing. You remind me of my roommate's mom. She's always so welcoming whenever I go to visit."

"Thank you, Kaylie. That's quite a compliment. I only wish Jackson appreciated me a little bit more," she teased him as she poured us both a glass of orange juice.

"You know I think you're the best, Mom," Jackson said as he jumped up to give her a quick hug.

"And don't you forget it!" she replied. "Speaking of forgetting, I hope you remembered to thank Kaylie for her help and to apologize for scaring her this morning. The poor girl had just woken up in a strange house and the first thing that happens is she's accosted by my cranky boy in the hallway."

I giggled at her comment, happy to hear that she didn't think poorly of me after finding us in Jackson's room. "Nope, he hasn't actually gotten around to that part yet," I said. "He's mentioned owing me an apology, if that helps any."

"Oh, you'll get your apology. Don't worry about that. And a thank-you for all of your help," he said with a gleam in his eye that I just didn't trust.

"Perfect! Now I need to head out or else. I hope this isn't the last time I get to see you, Kaylie," she said as she bent down to give me a quick kiss on the cheek. "And you better behave, Jackson. Don't go making her think that your mom didn't raise you right."

"Even if he doesn't, I already know you raised Aubrey right, so it will only reflect badly on Jackson and not you," I joked as she walked out the door.

"If you're friends with Aubrey, how come I haven't seen you around before?" Jackson asked between bites of his breakfast.

"We've only really gotten to know each other recently. We have a dance class together."

"And does my sister know you're also friends with Sasha? Because I'm pretty sure that would go over with her like a lead balloon," he said, picking up his plate to take it to the sink. He gestured at my empty one and grabbed it on the way.

"I never said I was friends with Sasha," I pointed out as I helped him clear the rest of the table. "She's just my neighbor at the dorm."

"Well aren't you just a good girl then?" he asked. "You run to the rescue of someone who I'm sure is the neighbor from hell and you help strange guys make it home to their parents when they get sick in the bar."

"I didn't run to Sasha's rescue. I came over to ask you guys to keep it down so I could get some sleep and stayed when I realized that it was never going to happen anyway until you left," I argued.

"And do you pick up strangers in bars often?"

"You weren't a stranger, Jackson," I reminded him. "And I didn't pick you up."

"You got in my truck, came to my house, and slept in my shirt. Seems pretty damn close to picking me up in a bar. We just missed out on the really good parts."

"No, the really good part is going to be you thanking me and apologizing for accosting me in the hallway before you take me back to the dorm, where I can pretend this morning never happened."

"Hmmmm," he murmured. "I think I can do better than a half-assed apology like that. What kind of brother would I be if I didn't treat a friend of Aubrey's right? I'll just have to think of something on the ride back. You ready to go?"

"Yes, absolutely! Please, let's go right now!"

CHAPTER 4

JACKSON

I wasn't sure what to think about this Kaylie chick. I'd thought she was hot when I'd thrown Sasha's door open and found her standing on the other side, glaring at me in her pajamas. The fact that I'd even noticed her in the middle of that clusterfuck was kind of a surprise. Then, when I realized it was her legs I was staring at from underneath my t-shirt this morning, I swear I was tempted to toss her on the bed and bury my cock deep inside her. No way in hell was I actually going to do it, but I was pissed at the thought that I might have gotten wasted enough to bring her to my parents' house and then not been able to remember anything about the whole night.

When my mom explained what had really happened, I wasn't sure if I should be relieved that I hadn't gotten in her panties the night before or frustrated because that meant I might have blown my chance to get in them after how I'd acted this morning. Which didn't make sense because I usually couldn't care less who ended up in my bed as long as they followed the rules while they were there. I liked being in charge, in control. Only she'd seen me at some of my worst moments lately, and now the tables were turned. She had the power because she'd done me a favor when I needed it.

I glanced over to see Kaylie looking out the window. She seemed pretty immune to my charm. That alone was enough to make me interested in her, since all the other girls on campus seemed so easy to get into bed. Or maybe she had decided that I was a total douche since she'd seen me yelling at Sasha and then I'd treated her like shit this morning. My mom was right, dammit. I did owe her an apology and a thank-you. And one of the things I really hated was owing anyone anything.

"So what exactly happened last night?" I asked to get her attention.

"Nothing bad. Char thought she'd over-served you, but I realized you were sick. I sent Aubrey a text and she thought it would be best if I drove you back to your parents' place. It was late, I was really tired, and your mom suggested that I spend the night. You were awake and alert for everything after that," she listed out for me.

"And you drove my truck?"

That question caught her attention, and she turned in her seat to face me. "Yup. I think that was the best part. You didn't seem too happy to give up the car keys at first, but you were feeling so bad that you just climbed in and fell asleep while I was driving, baby boy."

"That's pretty bold, using my mom's nickname for me. You sure you want to go there?" I asked.

She laughed at my warning. "I don't know, Jackson. Are you going to call me little girl anymore? Because even when you were sick you still managed to call me that. Turnabout is fair play and all that."

"See, now that's where you're wrong. I'm not really into being fair. I like the odds stacked in my favor."

"I guess it's just too damn bad for you that they aren't then," she teased.

"That's the nice thing about odds, Kaylie. They can change at any time."

"It doesn't mean they will shift into your favor though," she pointed out.

"Is that a challenge?" I asked, sorely tempted to prove to her that I could come out on top with this thing that was simmering between us. Because I certainly wouldn't mind getting literally on top of her. She was a tempting sight riding next to me, even in her Roost t-shirt and jeans with no makeup on. There was just something about her that pulled me in.

"Nope," she answered.

"That's it? You don't have anything else to add?" Usually girls prattled on endlessly, trying to get my attention.

"Yeah," she said before pointing to the left. "You're gonna want to turn here for my dorm. Just in case you forgot."

Damn, she cracked me the fuck up. She really didn't seem to care what she said, how she looked, or if I was flirting with her.

"No backseat driving allowed in my truck, Kaylie."

"I'm not even in the back seat. Besides, that was navigating," she said with a big grin on her pretty face.

"Smartass. I know where your dorm is."

"Better a smartass than a dumbass," she giggled.

I couldn't help but laugh at her comment. "I don't think I've heard it put that way before, but I guess it's true," I said as I pulled into the parking lot.

"That's what my dad used to always say to my mom when she got sassy with him," she whispered. She'd turned back to look out the window again, her arms wrapped around her body.

"Used to?" I asked, startled by how fragile she suddenly looked. The sassy girl from a moment ago had disappeared in a blink of an eye with the mention of her parents.

"Yeah," she answered, not offering any more details.

I parked in front of her dorm and twisted my body so I was facing her before unlocking the doors so she could get out. "Well then I better not be a dumbass anymore. Because I'm pretty sure that's what you think I am."

That seemed to startle her back to the present. "Not at all!"

"Okay, how about a douche then? You didn't have to come to my rescue last night, but you did. And I appreciate it. The last thing you deserved after helping me out was me jumping to the wrong idea about what happened and trying to kick you out before anyone else saw you. I'm sorry about that by the way."

"It's okay. I get that you were really out of it last night and didn't know what was going on this morning," she said, completely willing to let me off the hook.

"No, it's not okay. I would want to kick someone's ass if they treated Aubrey like that after she helped them out. Then again, I'd probably kick hers first for driving off with a guy she didn't really know."

"I'd love to see you try to kick Aubrey's butt for doing whatever she wants."

"Oh, trust me. My little sis knows just how far she can push me. But that's beside the point. I owe you one, and I want to pay you back. How about dinner?" I asked.

Kaylie's jaw just about dropped at my offer. "Ummm, I'm not sure that's a good idea, Jackson," she said.

And now she'd shocked the shit out of me. I hadn't had a girl say no to anything I'd offered in a very long time. The weird thing was that I kinda liked it—this push and pull between us. It wasn't easy, but it was fun.

"But how else am I supposed to even things up between us?"

"Who said you had to?" she retorted.

"Me. I did. And my mom. Aubrey would too. You don't want me to get into trouble with my mom and sister, do you?" I asked, laying on the guilt.

"No, I wouldn't," she sighed. "But does it have to be dinner? My schedule is pretty crazy right now."

"I'm sure you can squeeze me in. My mom already did the breakfast thing, and lunch doesn't really scream 'Thank you.'"

I hesitated for a moment, contemplating his offer. "Fine. You can take me to dinner tomorrow night," she conceded.

"Awww, c'mon. Not tonight?" I knew that I was pushing it, but I just couldn't stop myself.

"I have a shift at the bar again, so that wouldn't work unless you want to do an early-bird special at the local diner with all the senior citizens."

"Yeah, I think I'll pass on that. Tomorrow night it is then. Pick you up at six?" I replied, wanting to nail down the details.

"Sure. Now that we have that out of the way, can you let me out? I've got stuff to do today before I have to go to work," she said, gesturing at the lock on her door.

I watched her climb out of the truck and walk into the dorm. Damn, her ass looked good in jeans. I wouldn't mind if my thank-you dinner turned into a night of me giving her something to be thankful for, that was for sure.

As I pulled out of the parking lot, my cell rang with my sister's ringtone. "Hey," I answered.

"Morning, Jackson. You feeling any better? I tried calling the house to check on you, but nobody answered."

"Yeah, I'm fine. Just dropped your friend off at her dorm and I'm on my way back to the frat house," I said.

"Ugh! I hate you so much. I can't believe that you were basically comatose last night and are perfectly fine this morning. You know that if I come down with so much as a cold I'm knocked out for days. So unfair!" she complained.

"You snooze you lose, sis. That's what happens when you're the runt of the litter," I teased.

"Litter!" she laughed. "Dude, you better not let Mom hear you comparing her to a dog or your ass is grass. And there are only two of us, so it's not like I'm the runt. I'm just younger and prettier than you."

"Since you mentioned young and pretty, what do you know about Kaylie?"

"No!" she yelled in my ear. "Not just no, but hell no. You're my brother and I love you dearly, but you know that I absolutely hate when you mess around with one of my friends. And I could easily see her becoming one of my few close friends. So do me a favor and don't go there, okay? There are lots of other girls on campus who I'm sure would be more than happy to entertain you for a night or two if you're ready to jump back on the crazy train again. Pick one of them instead. Hell, pick a few of them and have a party for all I care."

"I didn't say I was going to mess around with Kaylie. I just asked what you know about her because I'm taking her to dinner to thank her for helping me out last night," I defended.

"I know how you are with girls, Jackson. Although I don't know when the last time was that you had to buy a girl dinner first. Just don't go there with her, okay? She's really nice and I don't want her to hate me when you screw her and toss her aside."

"Damn, sis. Give me a little bit of credit here. I owe her one and am just paying her back with a meal, okay?"

"You don't have any credit left with me when it comes to my friends, Jackson. I have had too many girls try to become my friend because they want to get closer to you, only to come crying to me when they realize that a night of sex is just that to you and they haven't bagged you as their boyfriend."

"And that's why you should be thanking me instead of ragging on me about this. Any chick who plays games like that with you deserves to be used," I reminded her.

"I know, but Kaylie is different. She's nice and likes to help people instead of use them to her advantage. My being your sister didn't factor into our friendship until last night when she helped me out by making sure you were okay."

"I thought you'd be happy that I was taking someone like her to dinner, even if it was just to pay her back," I pointed out.

"Of course I want you to date someone nice, but you don't date. You just mess around. Besides which, she isn't the type of girl who has one-night stands anyway. So go sniff somewhere else."

"Jesus, Aubrey. Sniffing around?"

"Hey, you started it with the whole litter comment. But seriously, don't fuck up my friendship with Kaylie just because you want to get laid. Okay?" she asked.

"I hear ya, but I've gotta run. Got things to do and places to sniff. Talk to you later, sis," I said before hanging up on her.

I didn't really have any idea what was going to happen at dinner tomorrow night with Kaylie, but I was interested in her in a way I hadn't been with another girl before. I knew my sister didn't keep track of my sex life, but it was pretty clear from our conversation that she didn't know that I'd refrained from one-stands this year. At first it had been because I was focused on Lex being on campus, but once she and Drake had hooked up, I'd realized that it didn't hold the same appeal it had before. Sure, the sex was great and I missed the release that I'd get. But I'd spent plenty of time fucking around, and I wasn't sure that's what I wanted to do anymore. But that sure as hell didn't mean

I'd turn down a night in Kaylie's bed if she offered.

CHAPTER 5

KAYLIE

I crept into our room as quietly as I possibly could, hopeful that Charlotte had fallen back asleep after she'd gotten my text letting her know I was okay and had just fallen asleep last night since I'd been so tired. I hated when she was pissed at me, and I totally got why she was angry right now. I sat down on the bed and pulled off my shoes. I could use a little more sleep myself since it was going to be another late night at the bar.

"Don't think for a second that I don't hear you over there," I heard Charlotte mumble from under her covers.

"Sorry," I whispered.

She flung the blankets off her head. "You should be sorry! What the hell happened last night, Kaylie? You let me know you were taking Jackson to his parents' house, that you got there safely, and then nothing else all night long. You're damn lucky I didn't call the cops out on your ass."

"I am so sorry, Char. I don't know what had happened. I think all the craziness from school, the show, and work just caught up with me. I was waiting for his dad to come back and fell sound asleep on the couch. I don't even really remember going upstairs to crash in Aubrey's room. If I had been more than half awake, you totally know that I would have let you know that I was just going to stay," I apologized.

"You're lucky I had Aubrey's phone number handy. I sent her a text asking if she'd heard from you, so she checked with her mom for me," she told me. "If not, I seriously would be pissed at you this morning. As it is, I barely got any sleep last night."

I tossed a pillow at her. "So you knew all along where I was last night? What was up with the text messages then?"

"Oh, I sent those before I thought to check in with Aubrey. I wasn't even sure I had her phone number, but you did a group text when we all went to that dance thing. Now shush. I want to try to catch a few more z's before I have to be up. You know I need my beauty sleep."

"Well I was trying to be quiet before you lit into me," I reminded her.

"Whatever," she muttered back at me, rolling away.

I pulled off my jeans and climbed under the sheets. It was a good thing Char was so tired and didn't think to ask me more questions. I was pretty sure she'd have plenty of them for me when I told her that I was going to dinner with Jackson tomorrow night. I just didn't know what my answers would be.

****

The rest of the day flew by, so I didn't really have the chance to talk to Char about it. Or maybe I was just better able to avoid bringing it up to her. After my nap, I had finished up a term paper due Monday and then headed to the dance studio to get some extra practice time in. We had our senior showcase coming up pretty soon, and if I wanted any chance of getting work, then I needed to nail my performance. My aunt had disagreed with my decision to follow in my parents' footsteps by coming to Blythe. She'd warned me that I was ruining my chances of dancing professionally.

As much as I hated to admit it, I thought she might be right. But I didn't regret my decision at all. I'd been able to spend the last four years feeling closer to ever than my parents. Walking the same sidewalks they had back in the day, dancing in the same studio my mom had used, sitting in classrooms wondering how much they'd changed over the years… These were priceless moments to me. She might not have understood because she was still pissed that my mom had followed my dad here for school instead of going to New York. She would never understand my decision to do the same, but I couldn't help but want to rub it in her face if I got an offer.

My desire to prove my aunt wrong spurred me on almost as much as my love for dance. She could have made my college years easier for me by offering her support, but she'd chosen not to and left me on my own for living expenses. She'd had no choice about covering my tuition, books, and room because of the terms of my dad's trust. Their life insurance money had been set aside to make sure I could go to college if anything happened to them. My dad had been a planner like that, and school was really important to him. Which was why I hadn't just majored in dance. I'd done a double with business administration too.

Pulling a double major with two completely unrelated subjects and working to support myself didn't leave a whole lot of time for fun. Or boys. Char always told me that I used my schedule as an excuse to keep guys at arm's length. It was easier to pick nice guys who let me keep my walls in place and didn't ask for more than I was willing to give. Guys who were the complete opposite of Jackson Silver.

So why couldn't I get him out of my head as I got ready for work? Thoughts of him had popped into my head all day, even while I'd been dancing. Now was the absolute worst time possible to find myself distracted by a guy, no matter how sexy he was.

That didn't stop me from putting on extra makeup, wearing my tightest work shirt, and straightening my hair before pulling it back as I got ready for my shift though. I was checking my makeup in the mirror when Char came back into the room after her shower.

"Well don't you just look pretty as a picture," she teased.

I spun around in a circle like I was showing off a dress. "Why this old thing? I do believe you have one to match. Why don't you throw it on and we can pretend to be twins!"

Since she was a fair-skinned redhead with green eyes and I was perpetually tan with dark brown hair and eyes to match, Char just rolled her eyes at me before throwing on her outfit, which pretty much matched mine except she went for a less naughty shirt tonight. Mine said "Want A Piece of Ass?" on the front and had the recipe for the drink on the back. I usually didn't wear this one since it inevitably resulted in lots of cheesy pickup lines, but I was in the mood to stir up a little trouble tonight. I was sure I'd be serving a lot of shots made with amaretto, Southern Comfort, and sour. At least our boss would appreciate the bump in sales.

"What's up with the sassy shirt, hair, and makeup?" Char finally asked while we were driving to the bar. "Don't get me wrong. It's not that I don't love it, but it seems a bit out of the ordinary for you."

"I just felt like doing something different," I answered.

"And?"

"And nothing. It's just a change of pace. That's all," I argued

"Kaylie, you hate change. I mean, I totally get why with what happened after your parents passed away, but you are the poster child for structure and organization. You never wear that shirt, let alone on the busiest day of the weekend when you know there will be a ton of drunk guys at the bar. I know you too well. Something's going on."

Luckily, we were already close to work so she couldn't grill me too much. "Well, I kind of have a date with Jackson tomorrow night for dinner. Not like a date date. Just a thank-you dinner for helping him out."

Char looked at me doubtfully. "And your casual thank-you dinner that isn't a date made you decide to go for broke tonight and drive all the guys crazy? Clue me in because I don't see the connection."

"I don't know. Maybe a part of me, a very small part, kind of hopes that he stops by tonight. And after sitting across from him at breakfast in my clothes from the night before without any makeup, I wouldn't mind looking really nice if he does. That's all."

"Whoa, breakfast?" she asked. "You didn't mention having breakfast with Jackson. Or that he's taking you to dinner. And there's only one reason I can think of that you wouldn't have spilled the beans right away. You like him! I knew it. Winning!"

"Geesh, what are you, twelve?" I huffed.

"Sometimes, yes. But in this case, I am your super-intuitive roommate slash best friend slash co-worker who knows you better than you know yourself sometimes. And I'm super excited that y'all are going to dinner tomorrow night. Even if you refuse to call it a date."

"That's because it's not a date, Char! It's not like he asked me out because he's interested," I pointed out as I parked the car.

"Is he taking you somewhere to eat and paying for your meal after picking you up?" she asked.

"Grrr, you are so frustrating!" I grumbled as I got out of the car and slammed the door.

"Which is just another way of saying that I'm right and you know it," Char said, flicking my ponytail. "It's a date. With Jackson Silver, who has probably never had to take a girl to dinner to get in her panties. Oooh, boy! I'd love to be a fly on that wall. I can't wait to hear how it all goes."

I held the door open for her as we walked in, arguing along the way. "I'm sure there won't be much to tell. He asked me to dinner because it's what his mom expected him to do."

"Yeah, right. That boy could have found another way to say thanks that didn't involve spending the evening with you. Besides, you said he flirted you up a bit before. That means he is interested. Just promise me that you won't have sex with him right away. Let him savor the thrill of the hunt. I made Shane chase me a bit and look how well that's turned out."

"Jesus, Char," I hissed. "Keep your voice down."

"So uptight. You better pull B.O.B. out tonight to work off some of that frustration before your big date," she stage-whispered.

"Big date, huh?" I heard Jason, one of the servers, say from behind me as he tapped me on the shoulder. "If you needed to let off some steam, you know you could have just called me, Kaylie. I'd be more than happy to let you use me any way you want."

Jason was a huge player, possibly even more so than Jackson. We all swore that he only worked at the bar because it gave him the chance to pick up drunk girls every night. Not that he was ugly or anything and needed the beer goggles to work in his favor. But a guy who I had overheard telling his buddies that last call was like shooting fish in a barrel? I don't think so.

I pulled away from him and walked around the bar. I needed to run through my set-up checklist and make sure we were all stocked for the night.

"Gee, thanks for that oh-so-tempting offer, Jason. But I think I'll have to pass."

Char just laughed as she followed me behind the bar. "Whoopsie. I didn't realize he could hear me. Sorry about that."

"I should make you do breakdown again tonight as punishment."

"Ooh, punish me baby," she cooed back.

I pointed to her side of the bar. "Get to work, you brat!"

The first couple hours of our shift passed by without too much craziness as the bar started to fill up. I found myself watching the door each time it opened, wondering if Jackson would stop by. I didn't know why I thought he would since he wasn't a regular or anything. It was just this weird feeling I had after the look he'd given me when I said I couldn't do dinner tonight because of work. Like the wheels had been turning in his head.

After a while, it got busy and I stopped watching the door. There was a group of guys that were getting particularly rowdy, none of whom I recognized so they were probably in town for a game or something. They had that jock look about them, and they were definitely in the running for the most irritating customers of the night. One of them came up to buy their next round of drinks and headed straight towards me. I'd been lucky enough to avoid them so far, as Char had gotten them the last two times, but I guessed they'd taken her on her word when she assured them that she was already taken and not interested.

A huge grin spread across his face when his eyes dropped to

take in my boobs and he realized what my shirt said. "Hell yeah! I want a piece of ass if that's what you're offering. You certainly look like a hot one, darlin'," he drawled.

I played along. "Well who am I to turn a paying customer down?"

"Hot damn!" he crowed, leaning towards me over the bar.

"Ah, ah, ah. Down, boy. Just give me a second," I said as I gathered the ingredients for his drink. I batted my eyelashes at him as I chilled the shot in the ice shaker. I gave him a flirty grin as I poured into the shot glass and nudged it towards him. "Here you go."

"A drink before we head out?" he asked.

"Head out where?" I played dumb, as though I had no idea he thought he was going to get lucky with me.

"You know," he said as he gestured at my shirt.

"But that's what that is," I said.

"That's what what is?" he asked, not getting the point.

"What you asked for a piece of ass. And it'll be five bucks please."

He just looked down at the drink and back up at me again. Either the alcohol was slowing his brain down or he wasn't the brightest guy in the world. To make sure he got it, I turned around so he could read the back of my shirt. And finally the light bulb went off.

"Well, shit. That hardly seems fair to name a drink like that and get a guy's hopes up and all," he complained.

"But just think, you could buy a round for your friends and brag about getting them all a piece of ass tonight. How often can you do that?"

Luckily, he took it in stride and bought a round for his friends. He tried his hand at chatting me up while I was busy preparing his order. I had everything finished up and was grabbing a tray when he got quiet all of the sudden.

When I turned back around, Jackson was sitting next to him. He looked amazing in a bright blue t-shirt and dark jeans, but the look on his face and the tattoo peeking out of his sleeve made him look dangerous. And he was shooting daggers at country boy. Daggers that were then aimed at me as soon as he realized what my shirt said.

"Here's your round," I said. "That will be twenty-five dollars in all. The first one's on the house for being such a good sport."

He glanced at Jackson before handing me some cash. "Keep the change. It's just a damn shame that all the hot bartenders around here are taken," he said as he walked away.

"Jackson," I greeted him. "What can I get you?"

"Do you sell shirts?" he growled.

I wasn't sure where he was going with this, but we sold the shit out of the novelty shirts the staff wore. "We do," I said cautiously as I pointed to the display that was pinned to the ceiling above the bar.

His gaze skimmed over the selection and landed on one that just said The Roost with a picture of a rooster on it. "How about that one in a size small?" he asked.

"Sure. We don't sell many of those. It'll be twenty bucks."

He slammed a twenty onto the bar and just stared at me. I grabbed a shirt for him from the stash in the storage room, but he just shook his head at me when I tried to give it to him. "I asked for a small. That would be a little tight on me, don't you think?"

"I figured it was for your sister or something."

His gaze dropped back down to my shirt for a moment. "It's for you, Kaylie. I'd hate to have to start a brawl over what you're wearing right now."

"Wait, what?" I asked, stunned that he'd seriously just bought me a different shirt because he wanted me to change.

"You heard me. I want you to change out of the shirt you have on into one that won't make every guy here think that he might have a chance to take you home tonight. Unless you really are into picking guys up in bars even though you said you weren't just this morning."

"And I would do this because why exactly?"

"Because you don't want me to get into a fight where you work. Or you feel sorry for these schmucks who seriously think you'd offer them a piece of your ass after your shift," he murmured. "Or how about because you want to make me happy? Do any of those reasons work for you, Kaylie? If not, I am sure I can come up with more."

Char walked up, looked at the shirt between us on the bar, and took in the expression on Jackson's face. She gave him a quick nod before turning to me. "I can cover for you down here if you need to take a quick break," she offered.

She didn't say anything more than that, but I knew what the real message was. If I was interested in Jackson, I should take the shirt and change. Shane would have pulled the exact same stunt if he'd come up and found her wearing the shirt I was in now. She and I both knew that, and she was subtly letting me know what she would do if she were in my shoes.

But Shane was her boyfriend and had been for years. Jackson was just a guy who owed me a favor and was taking me out to dinner to repay it. Did I really want to let him get away with bossing me around like this? Then again, I was getting awfully tired of the comments from the male customers tonight. And this was why I never wore this shirt anyway. It was just too much trouble in the first place.

"Thanks, Char. I think I'll take you up on that offer. I could use a moment to myself if you don't mind too much," I answered before grabbing the shirt off the bar and stomping into the back office.

I nudged the door with my foot to close it and whipped off my shirt to change into the new one before I realized that Jackson had followed me.

"Shit, Jackson!" I swore while glaring at him over my bare shoulder. "You can't be back here like this. You're going to get into trouble."

"The owner won't get mad at me for coming into the office. He's friends with my parents and our bank carries the loan on this place," he replied as he turned the lock on the doorknob. "So I guess the only person I can get into trouble with would be you, Kaylie. And I'm not really worried about that right now because I think you should be the one concerned about getting into trouble with me instead."

I pulled the new shirt on and turned to face him. "See, here's the thing, Jackson. You're not the boss of me. You don't have a say in what I choose to wear. That guy at the bar might have thought you were my boyfriend, but that doesn't make it so."

"What if I wanted to be the boss of you?" he asked. He must have seen the confused look on my face, because he went on. "I'm not here for the drinks or the ambiance, Kaylie. I'm here because I couldn't get you out of my head today. I knew I was going to see you tomorrow and I didn't want to wait that long. I came to see you, and it turned out to be a damn good thing that I did because there you were with that shirt showing off your tits, offering up piece of ass shots, and putting ideas into other guys' heads"

"But I thought you didn't date?" I asked.

"No, I didn't used to date," he disagreed. "But I think that's one rule that's about to change. You said yes to dinner tomorrow night, so I guess I should say it's a rule that's already changed because of you."

"You're just taking me out to dinner tomorrow night because you wanted to thank me for helping you out and you're mom expects it of you," I argued.

"I may have let you think that to make sure you'd say yes, Kaylie. But that isn't why I'm taking you to dinner. I could have found a million other ways to express my gratitude without spending another minute in your company," he pointed out as he pulled me towards his body. "Flowers, a card, just about anything would have satisfied my mom. But I'm not worried about her being satisfied right now. No, you've got me thinking about my own satisfaction instead," he said before his mouth crashed down on mine.

His lips were warm, and he tasted like cinnamon. I felt his hands on my ass and let out a startled gasp. He took full advantage and his tongue swept into my mouth, tangling with mine. His grip tightened as he groaned and tilted his head to get better access to my mouth. The kiss went from zero to sixty in no time at all. He mixed it up with quick nibbles on my lips and sharp tugs as he sucked my tongue into his mouth. I grabbed the back of his head to hold him in place as my mouth strained towards his, and he chuckled darkly in response before pulling away.

"Mine and yours if that kiss is any indication of the chemistry between us," he murmured against my ear before kissing his way down my neck.

"Jackson," I sighed before taking a step backwards out of his arms. "I'm at work. I can't stay back here to make out with you while I'm supposed to be tending bar."

"I know, but I couldn't resist stealing one before you went back," he said. "That's the look I want you to have when you go back out there. One that says 'look but don't look too hard and don't even think about touching.'"

"For someone who isn't used to dating, you sure have the possessive alpha act down pat. And we aren't even dating yet."

"I've never felt the need to act like this in public before. There's just something about you that brings it out in me," he answered as he opened the door for me. "And don't think I didn't catch the yet at the end of your sentence. I'm just going to take it to mean that you've conceded to the fact that tomorrow night is a date. In fact, I think you could almost say we are dating already since we had breakfast together this morning. Technically, tomorrow night will be our second date."

CHAPTER 6

JACKSON

I stayed until Kaylie closed the bar down and waited to make sure she and her roommate made it safely to her car. I didn't like the idea of Kaylie being alone in the bar's parking lot this late at night with all the guys who had been drinking there all night. But I didn't want to freak her out any more than I already had by letting her know that I'd waited for her, so I watched from the convenience store parking lot across the street. She'd backed down when I asked her to change her shirt and seemed to enjoy the kiss, but I didn't want to scare her off with these possessive urges that were rising up inside me.

I'd always been a little intense, but it had never affected how I treated women out of bed. If a girl I wanted to bang wasn't interested, it was no big deal because there were always others. If she was with a different guy the night after I'd slept with her, it didn't bother me at all. In fact, it was a relief because it meant she knew the score and wouldn't freak out when I didn't want to go back for more. I certainly couldn't give a shit how they were dressed and if other guys noticed. The more provocative, the better.

But when I walked into the bar and found that hick

practically drooling over Kaylie's ass, I'd had to restrain myself from tossing him out. It hadn't mattered that she'd just been doing her job and that her shirt had probably increased her tips for the night. There was no way I'd have been able to last the rest of the night without beating the shit out of someone for making a pass at her because they'd gotten the wrong idea about her because of that damn shirt. Thank fuck that guy had thought I was her boyfriend and she'd been willing to change. Because I wasn't sure I would have been able to restrain myself otherwise.

That freaked me out because I never had a problem with self-control. I'd been doing karate since I was little and had always been able to center myself. But with Kaylie, I felt like I had been thrown into the deep end of the ocean with no idea how to swim. It was thrilling and scary at the same time. I didn't know which way I was going to get tossed next. I just knew that I was going to enjoy the ride.

I made it back to the frat house before I knew it since my thoughts were still on Kaylie. I could hear the music blaring before I even opened my truck door and realized that the guys had thrown together a party of some sort while I'd been gone. Not that it was unusual for a Saturday night at the house. Unless there was a big bash somewhere else with free booze, you could pretty much plan on us partying together. What was unusual was that I wasn't in the mood to join them, but I wouldn't hear the end of it if I didn't at least make an appearance. As the frat Treasurer, I had certain responsibilities to uphold, some of which had nothing to do with our finances.

I grabbed a beer from the kitchen before joining everyone in the living room. The party was in full swing with the guys chugging down beers like they were water and girls dancing in skimpy outfits to the dance music they were playing. The only time you ever heard that shit in the house was when the guys had girls over for a party. It just wasn't a party unless you had drunk girls gyrating to the music.

I wandered over to a group of my buddies to hang out when all I really wanted to do was drink my beer and head upstairs to my room to crash. I might have gotten over that bug from last night pretty quickly, but I was damn tired now. And I wanted some peace and quiet to think about what my plans would be for dinner tomorrow night. If I was going to take Kaylie on a date, I figured it was worth putting a little energy into it. Might as well make it worthwhile if I was going to break my 'no dating' rule for her. Because I sure as shit was going to catch hell for it from the guys, my sister, and other girls on campus once word got out.

Speaking of other girls, the sharks were starting to circle as the night wore on. I could practically smell the desperation in the air. It had been like this the last month or so once I'd stopped hitting on the girls on campus. They didn't know what to think about the change in my MO. Usually, I would take my pick of the girls at the party up to my room for the night. Or at least part of the night, because there was no way in hell I ever let them sleep over. I had my fun, made sure they had a good time, and then showed them the door. If I was feeling particularly lazy and she was a good lay, I might decide to go back for more the next night. But that was it.

You'd think after a month of me staying away that the girls on campus would have gotten the message and back the fuck off, but of course they hadn't. There were some who wanted to be the girl who got me back into the saddle so they could brag about it to their girlfriends. And there were others who wanted to cure me of my supposed heartbreak over Lex's relationship with Drake. That's not to say that I hadn't been tempted. Having hot chicks offer to do just about anything I wanted made it difficult to turn down their offers. My persistence in saying no sure hadn't stopped them from trying, and tonight looked like it was going to be more of the same.

"Hey, Jackson," some blond chick who'd wandered over to where I was sitting said in a breathy tone of voice that she must have thought was hot. "I'm Laurie. I was hoping I would see you here tonight."

"Yeah?" I asked. "And why was that?"

"Well," she said before leaning over to whisper in my ear, making sure that her tits were in my face—a sight I would normally appreciate but made me cringe a little on the inside tonight. "I heard that your tastes run dark and I'm in the mood for something dangerous tonight."

I pulled away from her a little so I could look her in the eyes. "Thanks for the offer, but I'm not interested."

She didn't seem to want to take no for an answer though. "Are you sure about that? I'm not wearing any panties and I just got a Brazilian the other day. I've been a naughty girl walking around all night completely bare. I think I should be punished, don't you?"

"Laurie, I get that you might have heard things about me that would make you think that I'd jump at that offer, but I'm going to have to pass," I said without even thinking twice. "But I'm sure there are lots of guys here who would be more than happy to take you up on it."

"I don't want one of them," she argued, starting to get pissed off when she realized I wasn't joking.

"Not my problem. And you don't want to become my problem tonight because it isn't going to get you what you want. Now move along to another guy or leave. Those are your choices here," I said bluntly.

Normally I could shift a girl off to another frat brother with a few smooth words before she even understood what happened, but I didn't want to play that game tonight. I didn't feel the normal temptation, only irritation. Luckily, one of my brothers must have realized how serious I was and pulled the girl away and out of my sight.

"Dude, what crawled up your ass?" Luke, another of my frat brothers, asked.

"Yeah, man," Zach said. "You're seriously gonna turn that down? You're gotta snap outta this sometime, and she sure looked worth some of your time to me."

"If I wanted to get my dick wet with her, then I would have said yes. Or asked her upstairs myself earlier," I argued. "But I didn't, so I told her no and she still wouldn't get lost. It just pissed me off. This is my house. I should be able to hang out with you guys without having chicks bug the shit out of me, okay?"

I leveled everyone with a stare to shut them the fuck up and headed upstairs to my room. Which is what I should have just done in the first place instead of letting my guilt for skipping out on yet another party force me into hanging out tonight. I slammed the door to my room to make the point that I didn't want to be disturbed and flipped the lock for good measure.

Ripping off my clothes, I felt my anger start to fade away as I dropped onto my bed. The second I closed my eyes, I pictured Kaylie in my mind and felt my dick start to get hard. Shit, I'd had a barely dressed chick shove her tits in my face and offer to let me spank her and it hadn't gotten a rise out of me. But one fucking thought about Kaylie and I was as hard as I've ever been before. What the fuck was up with that?

I shifted, trying to get comfortable, but my hard-on wasn't going anywhere. It was like I had taken a Viagra or something. I slowly stroked myself, squeezing my cock as my clenched hand moved up and down the shaft. Damn, I wished it was her hand instead.

I figured she would go soft and gentle at first, hesitant until I put mine over hers to show her how I wanted it. On the next stroke up, when I reached the engorged head, I caught the pre-cum in my fingers and wiped it over the tip. I could easily picture Kaylie bending over to lick that drop off with her tongue. I repeated the motion over and over, different pictures of Kaylie popping into my head. Each one was dirtier than the next. On her knees, hands tied behind her back, her mouth sucking me off. Bent over my bed, ass in the air, waiting for me to pound her from behind, her head tilted over her shoulder and those big brown eyes begging me to take her hard and fast.

I was so close to the edge as images of all the ways I wanted to take Kaylie raced through my head. My balls were already tightening up, and I could feel my cock throbbing. I wanted to hold back, to make the moment last. I couldn't remember the last time I'd jacked off to the thought of someone I knew in my head. Usually I pictured some swimsuit model or watched porn.

The thought of Kaylie laid spread-eagle, her arms and legs tied to my bedposts, leapt into my mind. Just the idea that I might be able to take her that way one day tipped me over the edge, come shooting from my cock and landing on my chest. My heart raced as I lay panting, stunned by the force of my desire for Kaylie.

I didn't think I'd ever wanted another girl the way that I did her. I wasn't quite sure what to think about it, but I did know one thing. There was no way in fucking hell I wasn't going to try my hardest to make every single image in my head happen in real life. She'd managed to catch my interest even when I was in the middle of that clusterfuck with Sasha before Christmas break when I shouldn't have noticed anyone. I'd chalked it up to my usual appreciation of a hot chick and pushed her out of my head when I went home for break and got my head back on straight. The bottom line was that I might not have had to work to get a girl in my bed before, but you could be damned sure that I was going to now if that's what it took.

CHAPTER 7

KAYLIE

I spent my Sunday doing laundry, studying, and running through my dance piece again a few dozen times. And trying not to obsess over my date with Jackson. Because he'd made it very clear last night that it was a date and not a thank-you dinner before he'd kissed the hell out of me. I swear to God, he'd melted my panties right off my body. If we had been anywhere else but the bar in the middle of a shift, I wasn't sure that I would have been able to walk away. Maybe my self-imposed dry spell wasn't that great of an idea now.

After the last guy I had hooked up with decided that he loved me and wanted to settle down after school and have babies and shit, I'd freaked out. I'd felt guilty because I'd thought I had been pretty damn clear that, while I'd liked him, I hadn't been in love with him and I sure as shit hadn't been thinking about forever.

Char had been right when she accused me of picking safe guys, but what was I supposed to do when even they weren't safe anymore? When they wanted more than you were willing to give and you felt like you'd kicked a puppy because you'd had to shoot them down? If you were me, you'd decide that the sex wasn't worth it and keep to yourself for awhile. Which sucked because I missed sex, and now it made me even more vulnerable around Jackson since my body was craving the pleasure it knew he could give me.

"So what are you going to wear tonight?" Char asked, interrupting my daydreaming. "Something hot right? You need to blow his socks off. Or his pants. I'm not sure why anybody ever came up with that saying anyway. Who wants to blow someone's socks off? It's not like you want to see his feet. If you're going to blow anything off, you'd might as well make it something interesting, right?"

"I don't think I need a hot outfit to get Jackson out of his pants, Char. I'm pretty sure he'd be willing to take them off regardless," I answered. And now I was picturing him half naked thanks to her suggestion. Again. So I couldn't really blame her for my mind being in the gutter.

"I'm sure you're right, especially after seeing the way he was watching you at the bar last night. And glaring at any guy who looked too long. Even after you changed shirts."

"Hey, that reminds me. I should be pissed at you for going along with him about that. You're my best friend. No taking his side, remember?" I said as I wagged my finger at her, trying to pretend like I was angry.

"Oh, please. You can act as outraged as you want, but if I hadn't offered to cover the bar for you, then you wouldn't have had the chance to make out with him in the back."

I decided to play dumb and act like I didn't know what she was talking about. "Me? Make out with a guy while I'm out work?"

"Yes, you. Don't think I didn't notice the way you were all mussed up when you came back to the bar, missy," she teased. "I'm sure changing your shirt could have made your hair fall out of your ponytail a bit, but it definitely wouldn't have smeared your lipstick. Or transferred it to Jackson's mouth. Or made his hair all messy too."

"Yeah, well I guess you were right about dinner being a date. Jackson decided that the way to make sure I got that it wasn't just a thank-you dinner was to kiss me. And that boy can kiss!" I exclaimed, thinking about last night and the way my body reacted to his.

"See? Another upside to choosing a guy with a past." Char she made a big kissy face. "You get to benefit from his finely honed skills. And if he can kiss good enough for you to get that dreamy look on your face, then he definitely has some moves he can show you in bed."

"Okay, okay. Enough of the 'I told you so's.' Help me pick out an outfit that will wow him, miss smarty pants."

We rifled through my closet and dresser and finally decided on a black skirt and dark red sweater that I paired with black knee-high boots. I liked how the skirt and boots drew the eye to my legs. Years of dancing had made them my best feature, and Jackson had sure seemed to like them when he caught me wearing his shirt. Nothing wrong with using what I had since I was pretty sure that I was going to need any advantage I could get with him. There was something about him that left me feeling off balance and out of control. I usually hated losing control, but being around Jackson was a lot of fun, and I hadn't had fun with a guy in a long time. I was a little terrified of the feelings I was having, but I guessed I would just have to wait and see what happens.

Before I knew it, six o'clock had rolled around and there was a knock at my door. I was impressed that Jackson had shown up right on time. Most guys weren't as punctual for dates, and I hadn't really expected him to be either. I was zipping up my boots, so Char grabbed the door.

"Hey, Jackson," she greeted him.

He looked amazing in khaki pants and a dark blue button-down shirt. I loved how the blue made his eyes seem even brighter and that he'd actually made an effort for our date. I felt less awkward about having dressed up since he had too.

"Char," he replied before looking across the room at me, his gaze zeroing in on my legs. It looked like I had been right in my guess that he was a leg man.

"I'm just about ready," I said as I stood up and started to toss stuff into my purse. As I was looking down, trying to figure out if I was missing anything I needed for the evening, he walked over to me.

"Here," I heard him say before a bunch of yellow roses moved into my line of vision. "These are for you."

"Jackson," I breathed out, stunned that he had brought them since he hadn't really seemed like the traditional flowers-for-his-date kind of guy. Maybe he looked like it all dressed up, but hot tattooed guy underneath was still the same.

He flashed me a smug grin. "Consider the thank-you portion of the night over and done with. Just so there's no confusion."

"My oh my, you sure are a smooth one," Char said. "Very well played. Why don't I just take those and put them in water for Kaylie so y'all can head out for the date part of your night."

Jackson reached out to grab my hand. "You heard the girl. Let's get moving. I wouldn't want us to miss our reservation."

"You made reservations?" I asked, a little worried that maybe he had picked somewhere fancy where I would look out of place. I felt sexy in my outfit, but I hadn't picked it with a super nice restaurant in mind. It was easy to forget that he came from money since he didn't act like it. "Where are we going? Am I dressed okay for it?"

"No, you're not dressed okay," he answered and my heart dropped. "You look fucking amazing. So beyond okay that I'll have to stick close to you all night just to make sure that other guys know you're with me."

I couldn't stop myself from beaming at his compliment. He was damn good at this. It was hard to remember that most guys would say just about anything to score. "I'm not sure if I should trust you," I said as we walked to his truck. "Are you being genuine, or are you just putting on an act to get so you can get me into bed?"

Jackson stopped and turned to me so that he could stare straight in my eyes as he answered my question. "One thing you can be damn sure about, Kaylie, is that I won't ever lie to you. What you see is what you get with me, okay?" he asked. When I nodded that I understood, he continued. "I know this might piss you off because it makes me sound like a douche, but I don't need to put on an act if I want a piece of ass. The real kind. Not the drink. If that's all I was interested in, there are other girls on campus who would give it up if I looked their way. No need for dinner. No compliments on how they look."

I pulled away from him a little, but he wouldn't let me get far. "You're right. That does make you sound like a douche because that's exactly what you used to be interested in. How could I possibly think that I'm any different to you than all those girls? That if I decide to let this thing between us run its course that you won't disappear the second the sheets get cold?"

"You're already different. I've never taken any of them to dinner. I sure as shit didn't bring them flowers or think about what I was going to wear if I saw them. If that's not enough for you, then I'll just have to work harder to convince you that I'm not in this just to get into your panties."

"I'm not very good at trusting people to stay around," I admitted.

"Neither of us knows what's going to happen here. We don't know each other well enough yet. But I do know that I was willing to risk Aubrey's wrath just by taking you to dinner tonight. She'd have my balls if I banged you and walked away the next morning. That's one worry you can cross off your list."

"You talked to your sister?" I asked, feeling a little better about the night and his intentions if that was true.

"If by talking you mean that she grilled me, then yes."

"Okay," I whispered and reached up to kiss him on the cheek.

He wrapped his arms around me to hug me tight. "Right, let's get date number two started. I'm starving!"

We made it to the truck, and he bundled me inside before getting in himself. I watched him as he started the engine and pulled out of the parking lot. It was hard to believe that I was on a date with Jackson. If someone had told me that this would happen a month ago, I would have laughed my ass off at the idea because he was such a player. A week ago, I would have said no way because I couldn't have imagined him being interested in me. Now, I was just happy to be here with him and a little scared by how he made me feel.

"So where are you taking me?" I asked since he had not answered the question earlier.

"How do you feel about Japanese food? I wanted to take you to one of my favorite places. It's a Teppan grill, but it has sushi too," he answered, sounding like an excited kid.

"You're favorite place, huh?" I teased.

"Yup. Good food and lots of it. Plus the chefs put on a bit

of a show while they're cooking. My parents used to take us there for my birthday when I was younger, and it's always been kind of a special place for me."

I was touched that he wanted to bring me to somewhere that meant something to him. He was already scoring major points with me tonight, and the date had barely started. I definitely needed to stay on my toes around him before I did something stupid like falling hard for him. So I just smiled in response and fiddled with the radio. I wasn't surprised to find it set to an XM station that was all about rock 'n' roll. I let the music roll over me and enjoyed the ride to the restaurant. We got there pretty fast, and it was quickly obvious that Jackson hadn't been exaggerating about coming here before.

"Jackson, welcome back," the hostess greeted us with a big smile. She grabbed two menus and walked us to a station in the corner where nobody else was seated. It was odd because all the other ones were packed with people. "Your waiter will be with you shortly," she said before walking away.

She wasn't kidding either. The waiter showed up before I could even get my coat settled on the chair. He had a tray with a two white containers, glasses, and cups on it that he placed in front of us. I easily recognized the first as a teapot but wasn't sure about the other flask-like one he had brought.

"What's this?" I asked Jackson.

"Sake. You can't experience Japanese food without trying it," he answered as he poured us each a drink. I took a small sip, not sure what to expect. "What do you think?"

"I've never tried it before, but it's good. Different than I expected since the only time I've ever seen was it in sake bombs at the bar before."

"Yeah, I'm pretty sure comparing the sake you serve at the bar to this is like comparing Popov vodka to Ketel One," he explained.

As I sipped my sake, the chef rolled a cart to the table. I looked around the restaurant, surprised to see him at our table already. Nobody else had been seated with us, which was really strange. We also hadn't ordered, but he seemed to have everything with him to make our dinner.

Jackson must have noticed my confused expression because he nodded his head at the chef before leaning towards me so he could whisper in my ear. "I hope you don't mind, but I asked for a favor when I made the reservation."

Goose bumps traveled up my spine at the feel of his hot breath against my ear. "What kind of favor?"

"The kind where I get to enjoy my favorite restaurant with you all to myself. I didn't want to share a table with a bunch of strangers."

I nodded my head towards the chef, who had started to prepare the grill in front of us. "And how does he know what I want to order?"

"I didn't want them to be out any money for letting me have a table to myself on the busiest night of the week, so I ordered a few different dinners for each of us. This way we can enjoy ourselves without anyone interrupting us. And you get to try a little bit of anything that sounds good to you. It's a win-win."

And there he went shocking the hell out of me again. I glanced at the chef's cart again and realized exactly how much food there was on it. "What about all the leftovers? There's no way the two of us are going to be able to eat all of that."

"Ditching leftover food is an easy problem to solve. You can take some back to your roommate, and I'm sure the guys at the house will devour anything I bring back to them. And this way you can have as much of anything you really like as you want."

I peeked at the grill, where the chef was preparing a gigantic mound of fried rice and eight sets of what looked like a shrimp appetizer of some kind. "You really do mean as much as I want. That's a ton of food."

He grinned at me and a slight blush crept up his chiseled cheekbones. "I might have gone a little overboard."

I reached out and place my hand over his. "No, you went exactly the perfect amount overboard. This was a very cool thing to do, Jackson."

He nodded before he grabbed his sake and gulped down the rest. "How about more sake?"

"I don't know. Did you order eight servings of that, too?" I teased him.

"Nah. I thought about it but then I wouldn't be able to drive you home," he said, shrugging his broad shoulders. "Hell, neither of us would even remember this date if we drank that much."

"And this is where I should admit to something. I know I'm a bartender, so this will probably shock you, but I hardly ever drink. I would say I make for a cheap date, but you've pretty much proven that wrong with all of this."

"Then I guess it's a good thing you can drink all the tea you want." He poured me a cup and put it by my plate. "You don't have to finish the sake if you don't want it."

"No, I really like how warm it makes me feel," I giggled.

"We better get some food into you," he said as he handed my plate to the chef so he could pile some shrimp on it before giving him his own plate. I really liked how it felt when he did small things like that—pouring me drinks and getting me food.

"Delicious," I declared as I took my first bite. I enjoyed the whole meal, tasting a little bit of anything that caught my eye. He really had ordered some of everything. We had chicken, two different kinds of steak, more shrimp, and lobster to go with the rice and vegetables. The chef made a volcano with an onion that he set on fire and kept doing tricks like tossing shrimp shells into his chef's hat. It was really entertaining and the food was amazing. It was absolutely the best dinner date I could ever remember having.

"I'm so full," I said as I rubbed my stomach, trying to get comfortable. I really had eaten too much.

My sweater rode up a little and Jackson's gaze landed on my bare skin. "Here, let me help with that." He reached over to move my hand out of the way and replace it with his. His warmth seeped into my skin as he gently rubbed in circles.

"Jackson," I murmured, lost in the feeling of his touch.

"Kaylie?"

"Yeah," I said drowsily.

"Ready for the next part of our date?"

My eyes popped open at his question. "Next part?"

"I thought we'd take a little detour on the way back to campus. You game?"

"If your detour is as good as the rest of the night has been, then count me in," I answered.

The waiter boxed up all the leftovers and put them into a couple bags for us to take. Jackson handed him his credit card and paid for our meal without even glancing at the bill. He carried both bags as he led me out of the restaurant to his truck and helped me inside. A girl really could get used to all this pampering pretty easily. Jackson might have been new to the whole dating thing, but he sure knew what he was doing.

He turned the music on low and switched it to an alternative rock station. The Foo Fighters came on, and I leaned back in my seat to enjoy the music. Jackson drove to the outskirts of town to the lake and pulled off the road onto a dirt path. We drove a few more minutes before coming to a summer cabin. He parked in the driveway and hopped out before I even thought to ask what we were doing here.

"C'mon," he said as he pulled me out of the truck. "It'll be fun, I swear."

We walked around to the back porch, and I noticed the sleds piled in the corner. I glanced down at my outfit and looked at Jackson like he was crazy.

"Hell no! I'd freeze my ass off if I went sledding with you dressed like this."

"I already thought of that." He gestured to the sliding glass door. "This is my parents' cabin. Some of Aubrey's winter stuff is inside. I pulled it out of the closet for you earlier today. Grab some snow pants, gloves, and a hat."

"But Jackson," I complained.

"Just once, Kaylie. Please," he asked.

"Fine! One time down and that's it. I don't really like being cold."

"If you're not having fun, then we'll stop. I'm not going to make you do something you hate, Kaylie." He gave me puppy-dog eyes. "I just thought you might like this. That's all. Give it a chance. You liked the flowers, sake, and dinner. Right?"

"Right," I huffed before stomping inside.

This was not how I'd pictured the end of our date. I never imagined that the infamous campus playboy would want to take me sledding.

I grabbed a pair of snow pants and slid them on, my skirt bunching up inside. I wasn't changing my boots even if they weren't designed for playing in the snow. I picked out a set of gloves with a matching hat and headed back outside. Jackson had already put on a pair of snow pants and pulled out a small toboggan.

"Ready?" he grinned up at me from the back of the sled.

I climbed in front of him and he pushed off before wrapping his arms around me. We went whooshing down the hill onto the lake and finally skidded to a halt. Jackson leaned back and tugged me with him.

"Look up," he whispered.

The stars were clear in the sky, twinkling brightly. Everything was so still and quiet in contrast to the heart-pumping feeling of barreling down the hill.

"Wow," I whispered back. "It's so beautiful, Jackson."

"That's why I wanted to share it with you. I thought you'd like it," he said as he tightened his arms around me. "Plus it means I have an excuse to get you in my arms since we're warmer cuddled up like this."

"So you even got Mother Nature to help you out with our date?"

"Hey, I'll take all the help I can get with you," he replied.

"I'm not sure you need any help at all, Jackson. Tonight was amazing. Thank you."

"You're welcome. Thanks for agreeing to come out with me, even if I kind of had to trick you into the date."

We lay there enjoying the moment for a while until I shivered a little, the cold getting to me.

Jackson let me go, giving me a little push to my feet. "It's colder than I thought it would be. We better get you back inside so you can warm up."

We held hands as we trudged back up the hill to the cabin, Jackson pulling the sled behind him. The way up was certainly harder than down, and my boots didn't make it any easier for me. Jackson had to steady me several times, catching me before

I fell each time. When we made it back to the porch, Jackson came inside with me unlike earlier. We both stripped out of our snow stuff, and Jackson hung everything up in the bathroom to dry. There was an awkward silence as I realized the date was drawing to a close, we were completely alone in his parents' cabin, and he hadn't kissed me yet tonight.

"So…I guess we should head back. I have a morning class tomorrow," I said awkwardly.

"Me, too," he replied as he strode towards me with a determined look on his face. "But I need to do this now. I don't want to wait until I'm dropping you off in front of other people."

I took a step back, and Jackson kept walking my way. My back bumped against the wall, and he rested his hands on either side of me, caging me in. I knew what he'd meant, but I couldn't stop myself from asking, "Do what?"

He responded by kissing me. The kiss started off slow at first, his lips caressing mine before he murmured, "Open."

My lips parted at his commanding tone and his tongue darted inside and entangled with mine. His hands moved to hold my head in place as he ravaged my mouth with his. I glided my fingertips along his back, enjoying the play of his muscles as he tilted his head to deepen the kiss even more. I wanted to get closer and clenched my hands to draw his body into mine. His hips rocked into me, and when I felt his hard cock rub against my stomach, I gasped. Jackson pulled away to make sure I was okay, but I couldn't speak so I just nodded my head and stepped into him so he would know that I wanted him to kiss me again.

He laughed softly at my action and shook his head. "I don't think I can trust myself to kiss you again knowing we have this place to ourselves."

"Please, Jackson," I whimpered.

"Fuck. You have no idea how badly I want to hear those words coming from your mouth, Kaylie. You really don't fight fair at all, do you?" he asked before giving me what I so desperately wanted.

My body felt alive for the first time in a very long time. My heart was beating so hard that I could feel my pulse in my neck. But he didn't kiss me like he had last time. This was softer, more delicate. And exploration of my lips with his as he licked the seams and inched away when I tried to deepen the kiss. He waited until I backed off before nibbling on my lower lip, his hands cupping my face. My eyes drifted shut and I enjoyed the beauty of the moment. This one perfect kiss from Jackson after the amazing night he'd planned for me.

"No more," he whispered against my lips. "Shit, Kaylie. We need to stop before I decide that taking it slow isn't a good idea with you."

"Maybe I don't want to take it slow," I said, even though I hadn't planned to do anything more than enjoy dinner and a couple of kisses tonight.

"What do you want from this? Do you want to maybe take a step towards a relationship? Or friends with benefits? Because you might not believe me yet, but I'm really not trying to just have sex with you. And if we do this now, how the hell am I supposed to show you that I'm different with you? That even though I don't know what this is, it still means something other than just getting off tonight?"

"I don't know what I want," I admitted. It was the truth. Until Jackson had stormed into my life, guys and relationships had been the last thing on my mind.

"Then we need to wait. Which means that we need to get the

hell out of here. Now. Before I change my mind, strip you bare, and find out if you taste as good all over as you do when I kiss you," he said before giving me a swift kiss and pulling me towards the door.

I was completely blown away. The campus playboy had just kissed the shit out of me and then talked me out of having sex with him on our first real date.

CHAPTER 8

JACKSON

The drive back to Kaylie's dorm was hell. It took all of my willpower to not turn the truck around and race back to the cabin with her. My dick was stiff, my balls had to be turning blue, and I could still taste her on my lips. Being noble didn't come naturally to me. It had been a new experience—one I really didn't appreciate right now, but I hoped like hell would be worth it later.

I'd wanted her in my bed more than once, and I'd figured she'd have had an excuse to run if we'd gone too fast. And wasn't that fucking ironic? I'd been worried about a girl not wanting to see me again after we had sex. Usually I hoped like hell I didn't have to see her after instead.

Kaylie kept giving me strange looks as I drove. "What?" I finally asked while she was looking my way.

"Nothing," she answered. "Just trying to figure you out is all. You really surprised me tonight."

"Surprised you in a good way like a present you were really hoping for on Christmas morning or in a bad way like finding out you picked up the flu bug from kissing me?"

"Definitely the good kind of surprise. You really went out of your way to make this a good night for me, and I appreciate it. All of it."

"Even me saying no to sex tonight?" I asked. I was a little worried that she might think I didn't want her or something crazy like that when nothing could be further from the truth.

She reached over to grab my hand. "Especially that, I think. It's been a while for me, but just because I'm horny doesn't mean we need to jump into bed together right away. I probably would have regretted it after. Your putting my feelings ahead of what would have felt really great says a lot."

I squeezed her hand in response. "Crap, Kaylie. You can't throw out words like horny right now. You're killing me here," I groaned.

"Okay, I'll be good," she giggled.

An image of me punishing her for being bad, smacking her ass until it was red, popped into my head. I wasn't even sure she liked that kind of shit, but I couldn't stop thinking about having her under my control. I'd enjoyed being kinky with other girls, and I'd always been willing to try something out if they'd asked. It had been more about what they'd wanted than what I was into, as long as I'd gotten off in the end.

But it wasn't the same with Kaylie and I hadn't even slept with her yet. It wasn't that I was less interested in what she wanted in bed than the girls from before because I absolutely wanted to know what excited her, where she liked to be touched, if she preferred sex soft and romantic or hard and fast. But underneath it all, I wanted to make her lose all control and trust me with her body. I had a feeling that with her it would be about trust, and I'd have to earn it before she was willing to give it to me.

I fiddled with the radio to give myself something else to focus on, anything but the thought of driving my cock deep inside her pussy. Luckily, the drive wasn't a long one and we were back at her dorm pretty quickly. The sexual tension in the truck had almost had me pulling off to the side of the road to kiss her again. But if I wasn't going to take her when we were alone in the cabin, I sure as shit wasn't going to start something in the cab of my truck on the open road.

"You don't have to walk me up," I heard Kaylie say as I parked the truck.

"But I'm going to anyway. This was a date, remember? And a guy should walk his girl to the door at the end of a date. Now if this was a thank-you dinner, then it would be a totally different story. I'd drop your ass off right here," I joked.

I enjoyed how her pretty brown eyes lit up when she found something I'd said funny. And the sight of her legs in that skirt and boots as she climbed out of my truck was hot. Add in that she was sweet and I pretty much had the perfect girl. Maybe that was why everything was so different with her—because I was getting to know her as a person instead of just a conquest. I couldn't help but wonder how many of the girls I'd screwed could have been more than that and I just hadn't noticed. Had I been so wrapped up in the idea of Lex that I'd missed out on other opportunities? Or was there something special about Kaylie?

We made it upstairs to her room while all those thoughts were rolling around my head, and I realized I was fucking up this opportunity by thinking too much. I opened the door to make sure Char was inside.

"Hey. Kaylie will be inside soon," I said before closing it again. I pinned her up against the door and looked up and down the hallway to make sure nobody else was around. "I had a great time with you tonight, and I want to do this again soon. What do you think? Did I earn a third date with you?"

"I'm still not sure about counting breakfast at your mom's as a first date, but yes, I'd like to go out with you again," she answered.

"Soon?" I pushed.

She smiled shyly at my question. "Yes, Jackson. We can do something again soon."

"Good. Now that I've got that out of the way," I said as I leaned down to kiss her again.

"Hey!" she protested, putting her hand over my mouth. "I thought you said you didn't trust yourself with me tonight."

I nipped at her fingers so she'd remove her hand. "I don't, but this is about as safe a place as it's gonna get since Char is on the other side of this door and anyone could walk up at any minute and catch us. And it's not like I can let our date end without a kiss."

"Ah, so you're going to kiss me so you don't miss out on a dating ritual?"

"No"—I bent my head so I could whisper against her lips—"I'm going to kiss you because I can't stop myself from doing it. Because I want my kiss to be what you think about when you go to sleep tonight. Because I want to be able to lick my lips and taste you when I'm going to sleep."

"Jackson," she sighed as her lips parted and her eyes closed, waiting for me to kiss her.

I didn't make her wait long before I started to place small kisses in the corner of her mouth and then moved across to the other side to do the same there. I sucked on her bottom lip before sliding my tongue inside her mouth. My fingers slid up her neck, and I could feel her pulse beating wildly. I nudged her head back to trail kisses down her cheek and across her jaw. I licked at her pulse point and sucked gently, using all my willpower not to bite down and leave a mark.

"You've got be fucking kidding me!" someone shrieked from behind us. "Get a room! There's one right behind you for God's sake."

Kaylie's eyes popped open and she started to blush. And then she looked pissed when she realized that it was Sasha complaining about us kissing in the hall. "Really, Sasha? People in glass houses shouldn't throw stones."

"And girls who are about to become Jackson's latest one-night stand really don't have any room to talk and shouldn't advertise that fact in the fucking hallway!"

"Settle down, Kaylie. I'll take care of this," I told her before turning around with Kaylie protected behind me. "Sasha, I think I warned you before about messing around with people I care about."

"Yeah, so what?" she asked.

"Leave Kaylie alone," I continued.

"If I had to avoid all the girls you've fucked on campus, Jackson, then there would hardly be anyone left to bother with," she argued.

"Kaylie isn't a one-night stand. I'm dating her."

Sasha's jaw dropped open at my words. "What?"

"You heard me. She's off-limits to you, too."

"But you don't date!" Sasha protested. "You always said you weren't interested."

"Things have changed. I wasn't interested in dating before, but I am now that I've met Kaylie."

"It fucking figures," Sasha muttered under her breath before glaring at Kaylie over my shoulder and stomping into her room.

Kaylie wrapped her arms around me and rested her head against my back. "Well, that was a great way to end the night."

"Let me know if she causes any problems for you. You shouldn't have to pay for my mistakes," I grumbled, completely pissed off that Sasha had ruined the moment for us.

"I might not like knowing that you slept with her, but I'm pretty sure she would have been a bitch even if you hadn't," Kaylie said as she stepped around me and placed a kiss on my cheek. There she went again, being so damn sweet.

"There are going to be other girls who will act just the same," I admitted, frustrated that my past actions might come back to bite me in the ass with Kaylie.

"Then I guess I'll have to learn to deal with it if I want to date you."

"If? There's no getting out of it now. You already said yes to another date," I reminded her.

"Well then there you go. I guess we'll figure it out as we go along. But you'd better get going so I can share these leftovers with Char." She waved the takeout bag at me. "And then let her grill me about our date before I can get some sleep."

"All right, off to bed with you then," I said, stepping away. I waited until she went into her room and closed the door before I left.

I made it down to my truck and all the way to the frat house before I realized that I didn't have her phone number. Shit! I really did suck at this dating thing. Getting the girl's number had to be the first thing a guy did, and I'd totally forgotten about it until now.

Going back to her dorm wasn't an option at this hour because getting in meant I'd have to talk someone into opening the door since it was locked. I glanced at the clock and realized that I only had a couple choices. I could head over there in the morning and hope to catch Kaylie before she went to class. Or I could suck it up and ask my sister if she had it. Which meant she'd ask me how the dinner had gone and I'd have to admit that it had been a date and not a thank-you dinner. I pulled my phone out and dialed her number.

"Hey, bro! What's up," she answered on the first ring.

"I need a favor."

"You do? What kind?" she asked.

"Do you have Kaylie's number?"

"Of course I do. But didn't you have that dinner with her tonight? Why do you need it?" She paused. "Shit, Jackson. Don't tell me you stood her up for a thank-you dinner and now you need to call her and apologize!"

"That's not why I need it."

"So if you didn't stand her up, then you went to dinner with her tonight. Why didn't you just ask her for it if you wanted it?"

Damn. Why did my sister have to be so difficult? "I forgot to ask," I admitted.

"And why do you need it anyway?" she continued without listening to what I was saying.

"Because I'm taking her out again."

And that stopped her dead in her tracks. There was complete silence on the other end of the phone for a minute before she responded.

"Jackson, did I just hear you correctly? You are taking Kaylie out *again*? The same Kaylie that I specifically asked you not to mess around with? And after that conversation, which you apparently completely ignored, you want me to help you out by giving you her phone number?"

"Yes, Aubrey. That's exactly what I am saying. I'm asking you to trust me when I say this is different. And to give me the number because I am your brother and I am asking you for your help. Something I almost never do, so it's gotta count for something here."

"Agh! You just had to pull the brother card, didn't you?" she muttered. "Fine! I'll text you her number, but if you mess this up and I lose Kaylie as a friend, I am going to be so pissed at you."

"Understood. Thanks, sis," I squeezed in before she hung up on me.

My phone chimed a few seconds later with a text message from her with Kaylie's number. Mission accomplished.

CHAPTER 9

KAYLIE

I hadn't been kidding when I told Jackson that Char was going to grill me about our date when I got back last night. She wanted to know every detail and was super impressed with what he had planned. Not that I wasn't, but I felt like I could depend on her judgment better to make sure I wasn't making too much out of the date. But she agreed that his buying out a table at his favorite restaurant, taking me to one of his favorite places, and convincing me that it was better to wait to have sex were all signs that I could trust Jackson. That he definitely wasn't out to sleep with me and walk away the next morning.

On the flip side, it took a lot of convincing from me to stop her from going next door to take on Sasha. She already didn't like her anyway, so finding out that she'd been a bitch to me about Jackson was like waving a red flag at a bull. I was pretty sure the next time they bumped into each other that Char was going to have some choice words to share with Sasha. Not that it was going to help with situation at all. I was just glad that we only had to live next to her for the next four months until graduation.

Damn, it was only four months until we graduated. What the

hell was I thinking to start something up with Jackson when I planned to leave town right after? I'd been so worried that he might have been using me that I hadn't even thought about the fact that I had no business getting into a relationship now. I needed to keep my focus on what was really important—finishing up with a good grade point average and blowing the judges away during the showcase. As hot as he was, Jackson would be a distraction and I could lose sight of my goals.

"Stop it," Char said from her bed.

"What?" I asked. I wasn't even doing anything. What could she possibly be talking about?

"I can hear you brooding from over here. Can you honestly tell me that you aren't coming up with excuses for why you shouldn't date Jackson right now?"

"Shit, Char. What, are you psychic now?"

"Kaylie, I don't have to be psychic. I know you. Jackson's different from any other guy you've ever dated. He's not going to let you keep him at arm's length. And I saw the way you looked at him last night. I don't think you are going to want to do that anyway. So I am sure that you are trying to find a good reason to back away now before you have the chance to get hurt. Don't do it," she pleaded with me.

"But I'm leaving soon," I argued.

"I know it's horrible timing. But look at Shane and me. We've lasted through four years of my being here and him being back home. You never know what's going to happen in the future, so don't borrow trouble. Enjoy what's happening right now and figure out the rest later."

"I'm not sure I like the way he makes me feel," I explained.

"That's because you've been dating pansies for too long."

"And he comes with a lot of baggage. What happened with Sasha could happen over and over again with other girls."

"Only because they're jealous. And it's not like you don't come with baggage of your own. It might not come in the form of a ton of guys you've slept with on campus, but trust doesn't come easily to you. Jackson is going to have his work cut out for him, and from what happened last night it sounds like he's willing to put in the effort," she pointed out.

"I know," I sighed. Then my cell phone chimed with a new text message.

Unknown: Thx again 4 last nite.

Me: Jackson?

Unknown: Yeah, who else would be thanking u 4 last nite? So I know who to beat up.

I laughed in response to his text and added him to my contacts list.

Char jumped on my bed so she could see my phone. "See? Totally putting in the effort," she crowed.

"Yeah, I guess he is," I admitted.

"No guessing needed, Kaylie. When a guy texts you the morning after a date, he's interested."

"Wait a second. How did he even get my number? He didn't ask for it last night," I wondered.

"The boy's got mad skills."

Me: Was surprised it was you because I didn't give you my number.

Jackson: I have my ways.

Me: Should I be worried about them?

Jackson: Nah, I'm sure my source will tell you all about it later.

Me: Your source?

Jackson: Aka my sister

Me: You asked Aubrey for my number????

Jackson: Yeah and I caught shit for it too.

Me: LOL

Jackson: Not funny! My sister's a menace.

Me: Nice to know you're scared of Aubrey. Might come in handy later.

Jackson: Haha!

Me: Gotta head to the shower and get ready for class. TTYL

Jackson: Fuck!!!!!

Me: Whoops. TMI?

Jackson: Give a guy a warning before you throw an image of yourself naked and soapy into his head.

Me: LOL! Sorry.

Jackson: Don't be. Now I've gotta take another shower and head to class.

Me: Another?

Jackson: No comment. TTYL

"Awwww, you guys are so cute already. And you have the goofiest grin on your face right now. You totally like him!" Char clapped her hands together all excited. "I feel like a fairy godmother and a matchmaker rolled into one."

I whacked her with my pillow before jumping out of bed to get ready. It was going to be a long one with three tough classes and a grueling dance practice at the end of the day, plus one of my classes was with Aubrey. I was sure she'd have questions for me after Jackson had asked her for my number last night. I just hoped that it wasn't too awkward between us if I was dating her brother. She was pretty cool. I didn't want to lose a friend over a relationship that probably wouldn't go anywhere with graduation looming anyway.

****

My first two classes went pretty well. I turned in the paper I had finished over the weekend, only to have a new one assigned that was due in a couple weeks. We had a pop quiz in the second class, but I had luckily spent some time studying and thought I did pretty well.

Now for the moment of truth—dance class with Aubrey.

I got to the studio before everyone else. I liked to have plenty of time to stretch before class began. Aubrey usually ran in at the last second, but today she showed up about five minutes after me, dropped her stuff on the floor in the corner, and sat down next to me.

"So have you heard the news yet?" she asked.

"News? What news?" I asked, confused as to what big thing I could have missed that would have stopped her from asking me about Jackson right away.

"Yeah. I heard some girl finally convinced my brother that dating was a good idea," she teased.

"About that… Are you mad at me?"

"Not mad, just concerned. I don't want to lose you as a friend, and if things go wrong between the two of you, it will be very awkward. But I tried to warn him off you and he wouldn't listen," she said.

"I'm sorry."

"So I'm going to guess that if I do the same with you that you won't listen either?" she asked.

"I might," I answered. "If you're really against the idea of me dating your brother, I don't have to go out with him again."

"But you want to?"

"Yeah, I think I do," I admitted.

"Then go for it. Who am I to deny you two crazy kids a chance at happiness? Besides, it will be interesting to see everyone's reactions when they realize that he's found a girl who's worth the effort of dating. I'll take my entertainment where I can now that I've taken myself out of the dating scene for a while. It's kinda funny that my brother decided to date shortly after I chose to take a break from it all."

"Yeah, I'm sure that will be loads of fun for you. Not so much for me though."

"What do you mean?" she asked.

"We bumped into Sasha last night at the end of our date. It was not a pleasant experience," I said before explaining what had happened the night before.

"God, she's such a bitch. After what she did to Lex, I wanted to beat the crap out of her. But no, everyone told me to let it drop. Not this time. If she pulls anything else, you need to let me know."

"I don't know. I think you might have to get through Char to be able to do anything to Sasha. She was so pissed last night and she already hated her."

"Good! Sounds like I need to hang out with your roomie more often. She's my kind of girl."

"You two really would hit it off. You should stop by the bar on Thursday night while we're both on to hang out. It's a slower night, but we'll make sure you're well taken care of," I offered.

"I think I'll do that. It sounds like fun," she said as the other students started to pile into the class since it was going to start soon.

I moved to the front of the room, getting ready to help lead everyone in warm-ups since I was a TA for the class. It didn't take a whole lot of effort, but it paid for my books. Plus, the teacher loved me, which was a huge bonus whenever dance companies were on campus because she always made sure I had the chance to network.

I led the class through all the warm-ups before she arrived and then joined them as we moved through her choreography for the day. Jazz was one of my weakest forms of dance, so this class was really helping to beef up my skills in that area. I wanted to be as well-rounded as I could so that I would have more opportunities come graduation time.

By the time class was over, I was drenched in sweat and panting. She'd really worked us hard today. I gulped down my water and tried to catch my breath. Aubrey waved when she walked out of class and made a phone sign by her ear as she mouthed, "Talk to you later."

I toweled off and leaned over to stretch again, needing to stay warmed up so that I could run through my routine a few dozen times as long as the studio was open. I needed as much practice time as I could get, and the room was usually open after our class. I hooked my phone into the sound system and set my music to play on a loop. The music was hauntingly sad and made me think of my parents. It was a lyrical piece that called for a lot of emotion, and my coach thoroughly approved of the feelings this one pulled out of me. I hoped it was worth it because I always felt completely drained after practicing it and it brought back the pain of missing my parents. But it seemed fitting that the piece I would dance that might decide my fate as a dancer would make me feel as though they were with me.

I needed to remember that I dance because I'm a dancer. This showcase might mean that I never dance professionally or that I'd be offered a job where I get to dance every day. But I couldn't lose sight that it was also another chance to dance. That was what each opportunity was. I couldn't think about what was happening next. It didn't matter what the dance was for. It didn't matter how much I doubted myself either.

When I first started to dance, I hadn't known that my Achilles tendons were tight or my legs weren't long enough. After a while, I'd been told that so many things were wrong with me that all I saw were all the imperfections. This was the perfect piece for me to go back to the beginning and remember what had made me dance in the first place. So I squared my shoulders, waited for the music to start again, and then I lost myself in the dance.

About thirty minutes had passed and I was halfway into another run through when I felt someone's presence and turned to find Jackson staring at me. He was seated on the floor just inside the door, dressed in workout shorts and a t-shirt. A huge grin was spread across his face, but his eyes were burning with desire.

"Jackson," I gasped.

"Those are some impressive dancing skills you have there," he complimented me.

"I certainly hope so. I've been dancing since I was four years old."

"When Aubrey mentioned that you had a dance class together, I pictured you doing the type of stuff I've seen her do before," he admitted. "But what you just did blows me away."

"Your sister is a good dancer," I argued.

"She's not a bad dancer, but I can't picture her doing anything like that." He got to his feet and walked towards me.

"She just hasn't spent as much time working on it as I have. That's all."

"No, after watching you, I'd say that you have a natural talent," he disagreed. "You looked like you were born to dance."

"Maybe I was," I admitted, thinking of my mom. "My mom used to dance. In fact, she might have danced right in this very spot many years ago."

"Really? I didn't know you were a legacy too."

"Yeah, both my parents went here. My dad got accepted and my mom followed him since they were high school sweethearts," I explained.

"Mine both attended Blythe also, but they met while they were students here. What year were your parents? Maybe they know each other."

"Class of 1991," I whispered, not used to talking very much about them and hoping that it wasn't the same time that Jackson's parents had attended. That there was no way they could possibly have met while they had been in school. My hopes were dashed at Jackson's next words.

"That was only a couple years behind my parents. We'll have to get them all together when yours come into town next."

I shook my head in response. "That won't be possible."

"I know we've only just started dating, and I'm not trying to rush the whole meeting-the-parents thing. I just thought it might be nice for them to meet up if they knew each other before," he explained.

I hated when the inevitable questions about my parents came up in conversation with someone who didn't already know what happened. I took a deep breath to calm the nerves before explaining. "No, it's not that. I'd love for you to have the chance to meet my parents. But that will never happen because they passed away six years ago in a car accident."

Jackson pulled me into a hug. "I'm so sorry, Kaylie. I had no idea," he whispered into my hair.

"It's okay. There was no way you could know, and I'd have had to tell you sooner or later if we're going to date anyway. We just got the awkward conversation out of the way. That's all," I reassured him.

"No, listen to me, Kaylie. I want to get to know you, and this is a big deal. Losing your parents as a teenager… Fuck I can't even imagine losing mine now let alone when I was still in high school. What happened?"

"They were having a date night while I was at a friend's house for a sleepover. They'd gone to dinner and were on their way to the ballet. My mom loved everything about dance. She didn't pursue a career in dance because she had me right after college, but she found ways to keep dance in her life. It was something she shared with me, too," I recalled.

"I'm sure she was thrilled that you loved to dance."

"She really was. Some of the best times we had together are connected to dancing. Even just funny little moments when we'd all dance around the house together," I explained. But this time, my dad had surprised her with tickets to the ballet, and she was so happy. There was no reason for the present. It was just because he loved her."

"It sounds like he had lots of reasons to love her."

"They both did. Even after all those years together, they were still very much in love with each other. I think that's part of what made it so hard on me," I admitted. "Before a truck barreled into them because the driver was in a rush to hit a deadline and didn't follow the rules about how many hours he was supposed to be on the road, I had a fairytale life with a beautiful home, two parents who loved me, lots of friends, and an amazing dance team."

"And after?" he asked.

"It was all gone. My parents were replaced by my aunt, who still held a major grudge against my dad for what she thought was ruining my mom's life. She moved me to her apartment halfway across the country where I didn't know anybody, and she limited how much I was allowed to use my cell phone and Facebook to connect with friends back home. But dance," I sighed. "She let me keep dancing because she hoped I'd go to Julliard and fulfill what she thought was my mom's destiny."

"But you ended up here instead?"

"Yeah, and boy did that piss her off. I decided it was more important to me that I was able to be somewhere they had gone before me than to go where she wanted me to be. I don't know if my decision was more about my parents or making her angry, but I don't regret it for a minute," I said as I squeezed him tight before stepping away.

"I'm glad you don't regret your decision even if your aunt was against it. Sometimes you just have to not take no for an answer and take what's coming to you. Never give in. Never give up. Stand up and take it. Sounds like that's what you did."

I was impressed with the way Jackson had put it. I hadn't really thought of it that way before, but he was right. "You know what? I guess it was."

"I can't take credit for that one. My dad says it all the time," he admitted sheepishly.

I couldn't help the laugh that escaped because he looked like a little boy right then. I liked this side of Jackson. He was more sensitive than I'd expected, more open. After going to the same college for almost four years with him and hearing about his exploits all the time, I'd never expected to like him this much. And I certainly hadn't planned to discuss my parents with him and end up laughing after. It was a topic I avoided at all costs whenever possible, but it hurt a little bit less to talk to him about them. I really liked that he got my decision to come to Blythe College, too.

"Are you all done, or do you need to stay longer?" he asked.

"I'm getting ready for our senior showcase, but I could probably be talked into being done for the day if I got the right offer," I teased. "I'm feeling pretty good about where my piece is at."

"I'm no dance expert, but you definitely impressed me. You tell me what I can offer that will convince you to spend some more time with me and you've got it," he said as he pulled me back towards him and nuzzled my neck. "I'm pretty sure if you leave it up to me I'm going to end up sexually frustrated again, but I'm free now too."

I enjoyed the shiver he sent up my spine. It seemed like his littlest touch did that to me every time. "Hey, that reminds me. How did you find me here? Should I be worried that you're turning into some kind of stalker?"

He chuckled at my teasing question. "I wasn't looking for you. I just got lucky and glanced inside when I was walking past on my way out."

"Ah, but what were you doing here in the first place? I don't think I've ever seen you in this building before, and I spend a lot of time here."

"Does that mean you would have noticed me?" he asked before spinning me around.

"You're kind of hard to miss, Jackson. I think all the girls notice you wherever you go, but that doesn't mean you get to avoid my question. Now I'm really curious why you were here."

"I was teaching a self-defense class," he said.

Now that wasn't the answer I had been expecting to hear.

"You were? I had no idea you did stuff like that."

"It's the first one I've done here. My sensei asked if I'd do a couple classes on campus when the school reached out to him over Christmas break."

"Your sensei?"

"You know how you said you've been dancing since you were four? Well, I've done karate for about that long," he explained. "But my parents didn't get me into it because they loved it or anything like your mom with dance. I was a bit of a handful as a kid, really full of energy. My pediatrician suggested martial arts as a way to give me an outlet for some of that extra energy. It worked, too. Karate helped build my self-esteem and taught me how to control my impulses. It's not all about the fighting. Just the opposite if you learn at the right place," Jackson explained earnestly. "I know people have a lot of ideas about guys who do martial arts, but I was lucky my parents ignored that crap and still took me there when I was little."

"Hey, slow down there, bucko," I said, putting my hand over his mouth. "If you love it, then you don't have to explain anything to me. I don't have anything against guys who do martial arts. No preconceived notions here."

He opened his mouth, and I figured it was to talk, but instead he licked my palm. "Mmmmmm," he murmured.

"Ewwww, Jackson!" I shrieked. "I'm all sweaty and gross!" I batted him away.

"There's nothing gross about you, Kaylie. I almost wish there was because you're pretty damn irresistible so far."

"Don't put me up on a pedestal," I warned him. "There are lots of things you'll probably learn to hate about me."

"Oh yeah?" he asked skeptically. "Name one thing, right here and right now, that you think I wouldn't like about you."

I wiggled one of my dance-shoe-clad feet at him. "That's easy. My feet. I absolutely hate 'em. You can't dance for as long as I have without doing some serious damage to your feet. That's why you'll never see me wearing flip-flops or running around barefoot."

"How bad could they be, really?" he asked as he glanced down at them.

"Horrendous. You'll just have to trust me on this one."

"Oh, I'm pretty sure I can do better than that. One day soon, I will get to take an up-close-and-personal look at them. I bet I can even make you like it," he challenged.

"Nope. No way, no how. Not gonna happen," I said, shaking my head vigorously. "These feet are off-limits. But the rest of me might be open to negotiation some day. And if you keep it up with all the cute guy stuff, that day might come sooner than you think."

"Cute guy?" he questioned, acting all offended before he picked me up and tossed me over his shoulder. "That's it. You've questioned my manliness. Now I need to show you just how macho I can be."

He carried me across the room and bent down so that I could grab my bag off the floor. "Wait," I said as I gasped for air since I was laughing so hard. "I need my phone, too. It's over there by the sound system."

He stomped over, staggering slightly as he pretended that I was too heavy a burden, and he swiveled around so I could grab my phone. Then he smacked me lightly on the ass after I had it.

"Now that's enough out of you," he said, rubbing the place he'd just smacked. "You're all mine for the next hour or so."

As we headed out the door, I couldn't help but be amazed at the fact that I was letting Jackson carry me away, literally, after only really knowing him for a few days. I wasn't sure what to think about it, but I was having fun so I was just going to go with it for now. Char was right. I needed to live a little. And I certainly felt alive around Jackson. It was worth exploring, even if it meant that I'd get hurt in the end.

CHAPTER 10

JACKSON

I surprised myself when I picked up Kaylie and carted her off with me. But damn it felt good to hang out with her. I had to do some quick thinking since I hadn't had a plan in mind. I hadn't been expecting to see her today, but something had pulled me towards that dance studio, and when I saw her moving across the floor, I'd been stunned. I'd thought she had been hot on our date, but seeing her dressed up like that had done nothing to prepare me for the sight of her with a leotard hugging her body and sweat dripping down it. And the way she moved—It sounded cheesy, but she was flat-out beautiful. It was like she'd been flying across the room.

I must have been a goddamn pervert, too. Because I couldn't stop myself from thinking about how flexible she must be. And thinking about her flexibility led to me thinking about spreading her legs as far as they would go so I could bury myself deep inside her body. I swear to God, I'd been walking around with a perpetual hard-on since I'd met her. And the way she'd wiggled when I smacked her ass—fuck!

I had to think quickly or else I was going to go back on my word and find someplace private for us. This waiting thing was a hell of a lot harder than I'd thought it would be. But the more

I learned about Kaylie, the more I thought it would be worth it in the end.

We got plenty of looks as I marched out of the building with her in a fireman's hold. After Sasha had caught us making out in the dorm, I'd figured word was going to spread across campus pretty quickly. She'd never been any good at keeping stuff to herself. So I might as well enjoy myself while we were the topic of conversation. I'd never really been one to worry about what other people thought anyway. But if people didn't like the idea of us dating, they'd better keep that shit to themselves or take it up with me because there was no way I was going to let anyone make Kaylie doubt her decision to give me a chance.

I dropped Kaylie onto her feet once we'd made it to the sidewalk. Looking across the parking lot, I had an idea. "Did you play little league when you were a kid?"

"No, I was too busy with dance classes. Why?" she asked.

"Because I have an idea what we can do. C'mon," I said as I grabbed her arm and pulled her with me to the batting cages. This was going to be perfect. I'd played a lot of baseball over the years, and the crack of the ball hitting the bat was a sound that brought back good memories for me. I was pretty good at it, so I could show off a bit. And it was a great excuse to get my arms around Kaylie again. Between this and sledding the other night, it seemed like I was going out of my way to find things we could do that involved me holding her. It was a pretty ingenious plan if I do say so myself.

I knew the guy working the cages from around campus, and he had no problem with giving me a couple helmets and a bat for Kaylie and me to use for an hour—although I hadn't appreciated the grin he'd flashed her when he realized who was with me. So I picked the cage the farthest away from everyone else to give us a little privacy.

"Here. Stand right here for a round and let me get a feel for the machine before you give it a try," I said, maneuvering Kaylie to a safe place outside the fence.

"Get a feel for the machine?" she asked.

"Yeah, I just want to see where the best place to stand is, how fast the pitches are, that kind of stuff. That way I'll be able to show you exactly where to be when it's your turn. I wouldn't want you to get hit by the ball because I didn't check everything out first."

Kaylie looked at the pitching machine and back at me. "So it's better if you get hit by a ball instead? And this is supposed to be fun?"

"No, neither of us should get hit by a ball. But it's better safe than sorry where you're concerned. Besides, it's not like it would be the first time I'd been hit by a ball. You can't grow up playing baseball without catching a few pitches."

I grinned at her before pressing the button to start up the first round. I could feel her eyes on me as I squared up to hit the first one, and I totally missed it. Major whiff. Damn, she was a distraction. Not the best way to show off if I completely missed the ball every time.

"Do you get a mulligan in batting like you do in golf?" she teased.

"Everyone's a critic," I responded. "I just need to warm up a bit. It's been a while since I've been to the batting cages."

"Mmmm-hmmmm," she replied as another ball whizzed past me while I was paying more attention to our conversation than what I was supposed to be doing.

I refocused my attention on the batting machine and waited for the next pitch. Taking a deep breath, I pushed all thought out of my head. The ball came rushing towards me and I swung with all my might. Thwack—a solid hit.

"Woohoo!" Kaylie cheered. "Nice hit."

"Thanks," I muttered, still focused on the pitching machine, waiting for the next ball. Now I felt like I had a point to prove and wanted to show Kaylie what I was made of. I hit about a dozen in a row, hard and fast. A couple of them might even have been home runs. I flipped the switch to pause the pitching machine.

"You ready for your turn, sweetheart?" I asked as I gestured her into the cage with me.

"Sure," she said, strolling towards me and pulling on her helmet.

"Okay, now you stand right here." I pulled her into place. Standing behind her, I put the bat into her hands, holding on to her arms so that she'd have it in the right position. "Hold the bat just like this, choked up just a little bit since you're smaller than me."

"Like this?" she asked.

"Yes," I replied as I ran my fingers down her arms, past her ribcage with a light brush of my fingertips against the side of her tits and to her hips. I used my knee to nudge her legs farther apart and tugged a bit on her waist to pull her stance down. "You want to keep your knees bent a little. Your arms, too."

"Arms and knees bent. Got it."

"Looking good. Now you just need to keep your eye on the ball all the way through," I said before stepping away.

"So pretty much the exact opposite of what you did the first couple times?" she teased.

"Yeah, somehow I don't think you'll ever let me live that down. Let's just see how good you do before you make fun of my batting skills. Okay?"

"Then let's get this thing started. I just flip the switch right there when I'm ready, right?" she asked.

"Yup. Sounds like you've got it under control." I walked outside the cage.

Kaylie turned to grin at me before she settled into a batter's stance and turned the pitching machine on. I watched as she did exactly as I instructed. She bent her knees, choked up on the bat a little higher than I'd shown her, and swiveled it in a little circle as she watched for the ball. When it came sailing at her, she swung with all her might and knocked the shit out of the ball.

"Damn, Kaylie! You're doing great!"

"Maybe it's just beginner's luck," she muttered as she waited for the next pitch. I watched as she hit that one too—and the one after that. "Or maybe you're just a really great coach?"

"Keep it up. Maybe you'll be able to beat my hitting streak."

"You never know," she replied before hitting a dozen more pitches. She flipped off the machine after she surpassed me and turned to grin at me.

"Did I bring a ringer to the batting cages?" I asked. "I thought you said you didn't play little league as a kid?"

"And I didn't. But you didn't ask if I ever played when I was older."

"And if I had? What would your answer have been?" I asked as she pulled off her helmet and came to me.

"Well then I would have admitted that Char played softball in high school and here at Blythe until she blew her knee out her sophomore year. She still likes to bat every once in a while, but she doesn't like to come alone so she brings me with her. And she might have given me some coaching in the art of batting."

"And you couldn't have clued me in before I tried to show off and gave you a lesson?" I grumbled.

"I thought about it, but then I wouldn't have been able to enjoy your lesson. And that would have been a damn shame," she pointed out.

"Yeah, it really would have been," I agreed before leaning down to give her a quick kiss on her mouth. "How about we make this more interesting since it looks like we're pretty evenly matched?"

"Hmmmm, I like the sound of interesting," she whispered as she kissed me back. "What did you have in mind?"

"How about this? We'll each do a round on the pitching machine. Whichever of us hits the most balls in total gets to claim a prize from the other?"

She leaned back to look at me and cocked her head questioningly. "A prize?"

"Yup. Whatever the winner wants," I dared her.

She stared me in the eyes for a moment before answering. "Okay," she nodded. "You've got a deal." She took a step back and held her hand out to me to shake on it. So fucking cute.

"Ladies first," I offered, waving her towards the cage.

I watched her as she squared up and took swing after swing, connecting each time. With each hit she made, I started to worry a little bit more about losing the bet. Luckily, she missed a couple at the end, giving me an opening to win this thing.

"I was in the zone there, Jackson. Think you can top that? You'd have to be damn near perfect," she bragged as she left the cage.

"I think I'm up for the challenge."

She looked me up and down. "I just bet you are," she said suggestively as she wagged her brows at me.

I stepped into the cage and waited for the first pitch. There was no way I was going to miss any of these. I wanted that prize. I wasn't sure what I was going to do with it, but fuck if I wasn't going to try my hardest to win it.

I took my time as each ball sailed my way. It wasn't about strength right now. It was all about accuracy. I just needed to make contact each time, and I didn't have a lot of room for error. I could feel Kaylie staring at me, but I couldn't look at her and risk being distracted like I had been earlier. I only had a few more pitches to go and I was going to bring this thing home.

"If you miss these, then I win," Kaylie said in a sing-song voice. "I wonder what I could do with my prize."

That split second of listening to her was just enough for me to miss the next pitch. I knew that she was trying to draw my attention away from the ball and to her, but I couldn't let her do it again. I was so close to winning that I could almost taste it. If I missed one more, it was a tie. The next pitch came and I tipped it for a foul, but it counted. Only one more to go.

I can do this, I thought as the ball came rushing towards me. I took my advice to Kaylie earlier and kept my eye on the ball all the way through my swing, my face splitting into a shit-eating grin as I watched it connect with the bat.

I dropped the bat and spun towards Kaylie as she came up behind me. "Wow, you sure don't like losing, do you?"

"I can handle losing, but I don't like to lose when it counts."

"And what do you want for your prize?" she asked.

"Not sure yet. And unfortunately I need to get going or I'm going to miss a meeting at the frat house. But I'm pretty sure I can come up with something good."

"Yeah, I'm pretty sure you can too."

I grabbed the bat and took her helmet so that I could turn the equipment back in. I grabbed Kaylie's hand as we walked to the parking lot, and I took her back to her car, realizing how close we had parked to each other and wondering how I hadn't noticed her car in the first place.

"Thanks for letting me kidnap you."

"I'm really glad we ran into each other. That was a lot of fun," she said as she got into her car.

I watched her pull out of the parking lot. She was right. Hanging out together had been fun. And it was something I wanted to do a whole lot more of in the future, especially now that I had my prize to look forward to.

CHAPTER 11

KAYLIE

The next few weeks flew by between school, dance, work, and making time for this thing that was growing between Jackson and me. He and I had developed a bit of a schedule, spending time with each other in the afternoon as often as we could and going out to dinner at least once each week. Jackson had been coming to the bar to hang out most Friday and Saturday nights when I was working. It was kind of sweet how obvious it was that my bartending bugged him, but he never said anything about it. He just kept showing up and making sure that I was safe when I was at work.

Not that he really needed to protect me from guys anymore since word had spread across campus that we were dating each other. Although his presence sure did help to make sure the other girls kept their claws in since he'd made it clear that he wasn't going to let them give me any shit while I was working. Hell, while I wasn't working for that matter. That didn't stop all the glares and catty remarks, but I could take it. I'd decided he was worth it.

Jackson had kept our attraction burning at a low sizzle, backing away any time we got too hot and heavy. There was no doubt in my mind that he was in this for me and not for sex. If he had been, there had been plenty of opportunities where he could have gotten into my panties with the bare minimum of effort on his part. Or he could have claimed the prize he'd earned from our day at the batting cages for something sexual. Instead he'd just told me that he was keeping it in his back pocket for later. But we'd reached the point now where I felt like tossing my panties at him to make sure it was damn clear that I was ready for the next step. In fact, that wasn't a bad idea.

"Hey, Char?" I said to get her attention off her homework so that I could properly judge her reaction to my suggestion.

She dragged her gaze from her computer to look at me. "Hey what, Kaylie?"

"I have a date tonight with Jackson—"

She quickly interrupted me. "And? It's not like that's unusual."

"And I had a crazy idea," I continued.

She jumped up and came over to me at that. "Oooh, crazy ideas are my specialty! Tell me more."

"Okay, but you have to promise to tell me if you think it's a bad idea."

"Like I'd have a problem telling you something was stupid. Please," she said as she rolled her eyes at me.

"Good point. I was thinking about putting a pair of panties in my purse and giving them to Jackson to tell him I'm ready," I rushed out as quickly as I could and waited for the explosion.

She didn't flip out and actually seemed to be considering it. "Hmmmm, that could actually work. But I don't think you can just put a pair of panties in your purse. You'd have to skip wearing them altogether to get the best reaction from him."

"Seriously? That's your great advice?" I asked. "Go commando and tell the guy you're dating that y'all aren't wearing panties before ya slip him a pair," I continued in a deep Southern drawl to mock Char.

"Yup, I'm pretty sure that's what I just said. And it was totally based off your idea to begin with, so cut the sarcasm."

"Sorry," I sighed.

"I get that you're nervous. But you don't have to do anything that drastic. You could just tell Jackson that you're ready. But I can damn well guarantee that if you did go commando and slip him a pair of panties at dinner, then you'd be in for the night of your life. He strikes me as the type of guy who would really go for that. In a big way. And you'd be the recipient of some major naked gratitude."

"You think so?" I asked. That's what I thought too, but I was letting doubts creep in.

"Oh, yeah. Like on-your-knees, lick-me-please gratitude."

"Ohmigod, Char!" I giggled. "Where the hell do you come up with stuff like that?"

"I don't know. It's a talent you just have to be born with I guess." She shrugged her shoulders.

It took me a few minutes to settle down before I could speak coherently again. "I like the sound of naked gratitude, so I guess I'm going to go for it tonight."

"Good for you. And while you're at it, wear a skirt, too," she suggested. She must have noticed my shocked expression at her suggestion. "I didn't say a miniskirt or anything. I don't want you to flash your vajayjay at the whole world. Wear that pink one that goes to your knees. It'll have more impact if you go pantiless with a skirt on. Trust me."

"And are you speaking from personal experience here?"

She gave me a sly smile before answering. "Shane may or may not have talked me into doing it a time or two myself. There is something so sexy about having a naughty secret like that."

****

So here I was that evening freaking out, minutes before Jackson was going to pick me up for our date. I'd sent him a text letting him know I would meet him downstairs instead of having him meet me in my room like he usually did. He hadn't seemed happy about the change in plans because he liked picking me up, but there was no way I'd make it out the door without my panties on in this skirt if we started the night in my dorm room. One of two things would have happened. Either I would have quickly thrown on a pair of panties or I would have told him my secret way too early in the night and we might not have made it out of the room at all.

Jackson pulled up to the curb, and I hopped into his truck before he could even get out to open the door. "Hey," I greeted him breathlessly.

He looked at me oddly before leaning over to give me a kiss and buckling up my seatbelt. I knew he liked to do little things for me, but I also couldn't help but notice that he always managed to sneak little touches into it. Like just now, when his fingertips skimmed my boobs as he drew the belt across my body.

"Everything okay?" he asked.

"Yup. I'm starving. Where are we headed?" I replied, hoping to divert his attention away from my nervousness.

"I thought we'd just grab some burgers if that's okay with you?"

"Sure, burgers sound great. Whatever you have planned is fine," I said as I made a waving motion so he knew it was okay to leave.

He headed to a local burger joint that had a burger toppings bar that I loved. They made the best burgers, juicy and perfectly cooked. And they had all sorts of stuff that you could get on your burger. I usually stuck with my favorite combo of mushrooms, cheddar cheese, banana peppers, and steak sauce. This time around I thought it would be best to skip the peppers with all the butterflies in my stomach right now. Which got me another look from Jackson as he sat down across from me in the booth once we were done ordering at the window. I swear, I couldn't put anything past him since he paid so much attention to my likes and dislikes.

I waited until we were eating before moving I excused myself to use the bathroom. "I'll be back in a second." Jackson just nodded and watched me as I walked away.

As I washed my hands, I stared at my reflection in the mirror and gave myself a quick pep talk since nobody else was around.

"You can do this. Hell, you have to do this. There's no backing down now. You heard Jackson when he said that sometimes you just have to take what's coming to you. Go out there and do exactly that."

I pulled my panties out of my purse and tucked them into the palm of my hand before striding out of the bathroom and back to Jackson. I sat down in the booth next to him this time. The plates had been cleared while I was gone.

"You want dessert?" he asked. "I wasn't sure so I didn't go up and order anything yet."

"Well," I drawled out before leaning into him so I could whisper in his ear, "I kind of had an idea about dessert."

"Yeah?" he whispered back as he nuzzled my cheek. "What kind of idea?"

I slipped the panties into his hand, which was resting on my leg, as my answer and waited for him to realize what I'd done. He looked down at my panties and back up at me with a shocked look on his face.

"Did you go and slip these off for me?" he asked in a hushed tone.

"Nope," I answered. He heaved a deep sigh at my response, so I filled him in on the details. "I couldn't have slipped them off just now because I put them in there tonight before I left. I haven't been wearing any panties at all."

As soon as I said that, he gave me a look filled with so much desire that I could hardly breathe. He jumped out of the booth, pulling me behind him. He rushed me to the truck and helped me inside. I felt his hand on my ass, checking for panty lines as he helped me in, too. He hurried around to the driver's side and revved the engine before speeding out of the parking lot. He still hadn't said a single word.

We drove in silence, and I wasn't even sure where we were headed until I recognized the signs. We were nearing the lake. He was taking me back to the cabin. As we got closer, he reached his hand out to trail his fingertips on my thigh, slowly inching my skirt up. Since I was bare, my legs instinctively closed.

"Spread 'em," Jackson growled.

"What?" I gasped.

"I'm calling in my prize from batting practice tonight. You're it, Kaylie. The best fucking one I can think of. The only prize I want. Now spread those beautiful legs for me and show me that pretty pussy that you're going to give me tonight."

"But, Jackson, someone could see," I argued, torn between wanting desperately to part my legs and my fear of someone seeing me.

"Nobody's going to see you but me, Kaylie. We're far enough out of town that there shouldn't be any traffic, and I promise to pull your skirt back down if I see anyone around. Please, sweetheart. Show me how daring you were to come out tonight totally bare just for me."

I took a deep breath, closed my eyes, and slowly parted my legs. I felt Jackson's fingers slide down the length of my leg and slowly inch the skirt up my thigh. There was a cool rush of air that warned me how high the skirt had gone before I heard Jackson.

"Fuck," he muttered. "I can't believe you really did it. My brave girl."

He gently pulled my leg towards him so he could trace the inside seam of my thigh. And then I felt the lightest of touches over my pussy lips. I'd gotten a Brazilian wax earlier in the week, so the skin was super smooth and very sensitive. I gasped and my hips inched up a little in the seat trying to get closer to his fingers.

"Shit, Kaylie. You really are bare. You're killing me here. Thank fuck the cabin is close by and nobody is there. Or else I'd be fighting with myself not to take you for the first time in my truck."

"Jackson," I whimpered.

"Shhh, it's okay. We're almost there, sweetheart. Just a couple more minutes," he reassured me as he continued to trail his fingers over me.

By the time we made it to the cabin, I was so wet and panting with need. I tugged my skirt down after Jackson got out of the truck. He came around to my side and lifted me out, carrying me inside. He kicked the door shut behind us and headed straight to the back for one of the bedrooms. He dropped me onto the bed and tossed off his coat. I pulled mine off too and started to remove my sweater next, but he stopped me.

"No. You're my prize. I've always thought that unwrapping presents is one of the best parts."

I watched as he dragged his sweater over his chest, revealing toned abs, broad shoulders, and his tattoo. I couldn't wait to trace his tattoo. With my tongue.

"But I'll get a turn to enjoy you, right?"

"Abso-fucking-lutely. I just can't promise it will be tonight, sweetheart. I feel like I've waited to get a taste of you, and I intend to enjoy my prize tonight. Often."

He pulled his shoes off and tugged his jeans down his legs, pulling his wallet out of the pocket and tossing a couple condoms down onto the bed. I enjoyed the sight of him standing there in his boxers for a moment before he knelt onto the bed and leaned down to kiss me. He took his time, teasing me with little pecks and pulling away each time I tried to deepen the kiss. By the time he moved to licking my lips and sliding his tongue in and out of my mouth in a motion that mimicked what I'd really like him to be doing right now, I was writhing in frustration.

"For someone who was in such a rush to get me here, you sure are taking your sweet time now," I complained.

"Patience, Kaylie. I've got you right where I want you, and I intend to enjoy every moment of it. Trust me when I say that you will too," he murmured against my lips before he leaned back so that he was sitting on his knees next to me again. He lifted my sweater up over my head and stared at the bra I was wearing for a moment. "I wondered if it would match the panties you gave me."

"Was that what you were wondering about?" I teased. "Of

course it does. I'd lose sexy points if it didn't."

"No, you could have been wearing the ugliest bra that had ever been made and you still would look sexy right now," he corrected me. "With what you pulled tonight, you earned so many damn points. But that bra adds even more."

It was my favorite. Black lace edged with red ribbon and a tiny bow in the center between the two cups. The panties matched perfectly except the bows were at both sides. "I figured it was a go-big-or-go-home moment, so I went with my favorite set."

"And one of these days, I want to see them both on you at the same time," Jackson said as he ran his finger underneath the strap, pulling it down my shoulder. "But not tonight."

He kissed down my neck as he quickly removed my bra and pulled my skirt from my body. Holy shit! I'd just realized that I was naked. In bed. With Jackson Silver! This wasn't something I had ever expected to happen to me, but I sure was glad that it was happening right about now.

"If that's what you want, then that's what you'll get," I promised. "It's my favorite set so I'm pretty sure you'll see me in them again in the future anyway."

"That's a dangerous promise to make, offering to give me what I want."

"I think I'm learning to like living dangerously from you."

"Well if that's the case, then I'm really going to enjoy my prize," he murmured before pushing me down so I was lying all the way back, stretched out naked for him. He trailed his eyes down my body and they darkened with desire. "Stay right there. Don't move an inch," he warned before he climbed off the bed and disappeared into the bathroom.

I heard a ripping noise, and then he came back moments later with what looked like pieces of a sheet gripped in his fist.

He glanced down to find me in the exact same position he'd left me in and flashed me a sexy grin before walking around the bed. He pulled my arm up a little bit and leaned over so that he could look me straight in the eyes.

"Do you trust me?" he asked.

"Yes," I answered without hesitation. He'd earned my trust in the time we'd spent together.

"I want to tie your hands above your head. Is that okay with you?"

Now that was a tougher question. I'd never really gotten into anything too kinky before, but I'd certainly heard the gossip around campus about Jackson's exploits in bed. And from what I'd heard, he liked to try things that I wasn't sure I would enjoy.

"I don't know," I answered honestly.

"Just your hands. And I swear I'll release them the second you ask me to, no matter what we're doing at that time."

"You're not going to hurt me, are you?" I blurted out. At his horrified expression, I rushed to continue. "It's just that I've had enough pain in my life already. I'm not really turned on by the idea of it in the bedroom."

He looked down at the floor and heaved a deep sigh before climbing on the bed to kneel by me again. "Shit, Kaylie. You never have to try anything in bed with me that you're not comfortable with. I know there are rumors that fly around about me. I heard all about them the first time someone decided it was a smart idea to share them with my sister. But I swear to God, you never have to worry about doing anything you don't want to do with me. Fuck, I'd be happy just to lie here with you naked," he said as he glanced down at the front of his boxers, where his very hard cock was pushing against the fabric. "Frustrated, but happy to be here with you."

"I'm sorry," I apologized. "I ruined the moment, didn't I?"

He lay down and pulled me into his arms. "No, Kaylie. If the moment's ruined, it's my fault. I don't know what the fuck I was thinking. It's our first time together. I never should have asked you about that shit tonight."

"Why did you then?" I couldn't help but ask, curious to know what he had been thinking.

He drew me tighter against his body and drew my leg over his thighs. I could feel his hard-on against my knee. I was now painfully aware that we were having an awkward conversation while lying here naked together. And that we were both still incredibly turned on. I sincerely hoped that the night wasn't ruined.

"I wasn't thinking straight. Between wanting you so badly, the whole no-panties thing, finding you completely bare, and fantasizing about having you like that pretty much constantly since we've met, I just went a little overboard," he explained.

"So the whole tie me up thing—that's what turns you on?"

He started to rub up and down my spine, a trail of goose bumps following the path of his fingers. "It's something I'd like to try with you, yes."

"And no pain?" I clarified.

"No, Kaylie. I have absolutely no interest in wanting to hurt you."

"But what about—" I started.

"Hush, Kaylie. I wish you could unhear some of the things that I'm sure have been said about me in the past. Hell, I wish I could undo them if it's gonna fuck up my chances with you now because none of it was worth losing this with you. Yes, I'd love to be able to tie you to this bed and explore every inch of your body while I have you completely under my control."

I shivered at his explanation. "Yeah?" I asked.

"That's what it would be about for me with you. You trusting me with your body. Knowing that all I want to do is bring you as much pleasure as I possibly can. It's not just some game with you for kicks. I dream about you. I can picture it in my head so clearly and it's so fucking hot."

The way he described it sounded pretty damn interesting, but I just wasn't ready for that yet. "Can we maybe work up to that stage and start off with something a little more vanilla tonight?"

"I didn't fuck up too badly?" he asked as he touch became bolder, his hand drifting down to my ass to give it a squeeze.

"God, I hope not. Because I am so turned on right now I can barely stand it," I admitted. I reached down and brushed my fingers over his hard cock. "And it sure does feel like you're up for it too."

"Damn straight," he muttered before flipping me onto my back and pouncing on me. "I can't leave you in need, now can I?"

"No, you definitely don't want to do that."

Straddling my thighs, Jackson leaned forward to whisper in my ear. "One thing you can bet on—I will do everything in my power to make sure you're satisfied, Kaylie."

And he proceeded to do just that as he kissed down my neck, nibbling at the pulse point and sucking my skin into his mouth to leave a light mark. He held himself over me with one arm on the bed while the other hand was busy cupping one of my breasts and rolling the nipple between his fingertips. He slowly trailed kisses down my chest until he reached my other breast. His tongue flicked the nipple several times before he sucked it into his mouth.

"Jackson," I sighed as I ran my fingers through his messy blond hair, trying to pull his mouth closer to me.

He let go of my nipple with a loud pop. "What, sweetheart?"

"Please," I whimpered.

"Oh, I will please you, Kaylie. I'm just going to take my time while I'm doing it," he promised before he switched his attention to the other side, leaving a trail of kisses as he moved across my chest.

I released my grip on his hair and moved my hands lower so that I could run them along his shoulders and back. I traced each muscle I could reach, my nails biting into him when he'd suck my nipple deep into his mouth. When he moved lower and nipped at the skin on my belly, I couldn't help the gasp that escaped my lips as I raised my hips off the bed. I was desperate for him to pick up the pace just a little bit. And I was rewarded for my movement when my pussy bumped against his cock, so hard and hot even through the fabric of his boxers.

Jackson lifted up to look at me, and the heat in his gaze made me burn even hotter. I wrapped my legs around his ass so that I could rub against him as I lifted myself up and down off the bed. I held his stare as I moved against him with his body towering over me. Even though he had me trapped under his body, I wanted to drive him as crazy as he'd made me. And based on the way his cock jumped each time I rubbed against him, I was doing a damn good job of it too.

"Soon, sweetheart. I need to get a taste of you first," Jackson said before he unwrapped my legs from his waist. He held my legs open, his hands hot on my inner thighs. As he bent over my pussy, I could feel his breath against my core. I was riveted by the sight of him as his mouth hovered over me. I needed his touch now, but I couldn't move my hips off the bed with his grip on me.

"Please," I begged again.

"Yes," he hissed before he flicked his tongue against my clit, like my words were exactly the sign he was waiting for.

He trailed his tongue down one side of my pussy lips and back up the other, over and over again, only stopping to give a few licks to my clit each time around. I could feel how drenched I was with need, his teasing driving me to the edge. Finally, he ran his tongue up the middle and drove it into my core.

"Oh, God!" I screamed, reaching out to grab his hair to hold his head in place and make sure he wasn't going to tease me anymore.

"Mmmmm," he murmured as he fucked me with his tongue.

He released one of my legs so that he could play with my clit. At the first touch of his fingers against me, I went off like a rocket. The waves of my climax racked my body, and Jackson drew it out as long as he could by switching so that his fingers were deep inside me as he sucked hard on my clit.

"Wow," I whispered when it was over and I lay limply on the bed, my legs sprawled and sweat dripping down my spine.

I watched as Jackson searched the sheets for one of the condoms. My legs felt like jelly and I could barely move. When he pushed his boxers down, his cock sprang free, long and hard. He found one of the condoms and quickly tore the package open with his teeth. Then he swiftly rolled it down his length and settled himself between my legs.

"I wanted to do this slowly the first time, Kaylie. But I don't think I can now. I fucking swear I'll make it up to you though."

I reached up to rest my palm on his cheek. "It's okay, Jackson. Take what you need from me."

And take he did as he slammed his cock inside me with a hard thrust. I was still so sensitive from my climax that I felt my body clench against him as he pulled back out to dive in again. He lifted one of my legs and brought it over his shoulder so he could get even deeper.

"Fuck," he groaned. "So fucking tight, sweetheart."

"Because you're so hard inside me, Jackson. I need more of you," I whispered to him.

His eyes lit up at my words and he pumped harder and faster, like a madman. My Jackson liked when I talked a little dirty to him, so I kept it up urging him on and telling him how much I wanted him, how good he felt. I must have really enjoyed talking dirty because another climax started to build.

"I'm gonna come again, Jackson," I whimpered.

"Yes," he urged me. "I need you to come again, Kaylie. Fuck, please hurry. I don't think I can hold on much longer."

He dropped my leg off his shoulder so I could wrap them both around his waist as he continued to pound into me. It only took a few more thrusts before I was going over the edge again, clenching against his cock and pushing him over with me.

"Damn," I whispered when I could talk again.

"Holy hell, Kaylie," he muttered. "That was fucking amazing."

I giggled in response. "You're such a smooth talker."

"Shit, I can barely think after that, let alone talk."

I rolled over so that I could look at him and noticed his tattoo again. I'd never dated a guy with one before, and I found myself a little obsessed over his. I traced it with my fingers before leaning over to kiss it.

"I really like your tattoo," I said huskily.

"Thank fuck for that because I enjoy the hell out of just about all of you."

"Except my feet," I reminded him.

"Why don't we do that again but slower this time and see if you're still worried about your feet after," he said before doing just that.

CHAPTER 12

JACKSON

Last night had been fucking amazing. It had been hands-down the best sex I'd ever had in my life, even after some of the crazy shit I'd tried before. Kaylie and I together were so damn explosive. I'd thought we might be based on the chemistry between us, but I'd had no clue it was going to be that good. I'd barely been able to hang on so I could get her to come twice that first time. After taking her again before we fell asleep, I'd still had to have her one more time when we woke up. Thank fuck I'd found that extra condom in the bathroom. I could have stayed in bed with her all day, exploring her body, if we hadn't had classes today. I hadn't even talked to her again since Kaylie had practiced her dance after classes and then had stuff she needed to get done before work.

Now, here I was, stuck hanging out with Drake instead of watching Kaylie at the bar because Aubrey and Lex had convinced us that we should do a guys' night while they did a girls' one. I'd thought I'd been so smart when I'd told them yes but that it needed to be a weeknight. If I'd had any fucking clue what was going to happen last night, no way would I have agreed to this when my sister asked me. I would have taken

Kaylie to dinner and dropped her off at work. After finally getting inside her, I just wanted to have her to myself so we could do it all over again. And again and again. I was so damn horny for her that I didn't know when I'd ever get my fill. For the first time in my life, this 'being away from each other all day' shit didn't fly with me. And wasn't that a fucking surprise considering how I'd never wanted another girl to be even be there in the morning let alone all fucking day after we'd had sex.

One night with Kaylie and I'd turned into a pussy-whipped idiot. Knowing that didn't stop me from being one though. Or from walking around campus with a shit-eating grin on my face all day, catching strange looks from my friends who couldn't figure out why I was in such a damn good mood. And there was no fucking way I was going to talk to most of the guys about sex with Kaylie. What was going on between her and me was different from the usual locker-room bullshit we'd toss around about the girls we'd banged. If one of them told me he'd do her or some shit like that, I'd probably kick his ass when I would have just told him to go for it with any other chick.

"You doing okay there, Jackson?" I heard Drake ask, snapping me out of my thoughts. "I didn't realize you were so into commercials."

Drake had talked me into hitting a sports bar to drink some beers, eat some wings, and watch football. The game must have hit halftime, and I hadn't even realized it because I'd been so stuck in my head. Totally pussy-whipped.

Not that Drake had room to judge me with how he was about Lex. If anyone had told me three months ago that I'd be hanging out with him, I would have told them they were a fucking idiot since he and Lex were together. It was a huge relief to realize that with everything that had been going on with Kaylie and me, I hadn't given their relationship much thought at all. Now he was just the guy who was dating my childhood friend and would get his ass kicked if he hurt her because I wanted her to be happy. Not because I wanted her for myself.

"Yeah, I'm fine," I finally answered. "Just got some stuff on my mind."

"Anything I can help with?" he asked before popping a fry into his mouth.

"Nah, I'm good."

Drake put down the beer he was about to take a drink of and gave me a serious look. "Hey, man. We never really talked about it, but I know I owe you one. So if there's something you need—anything at all—just ask. You've got a problem that I can help you with and I'm there. Okay?"

"Dude, you don't owe me anything," I said as I shook my head.

"I'm serious, Jackson. If you hadn't made me see how badly I fucked up with Lex and then got her to talk to me again right away, I don't know that I would have been able to get her back."

"I didn't do it for you. I did it for Lex because she was happy with you."

Drake looked down at the table before lifting his gaze to hold mine again. He cleared his throat before saying more. "Don't think I didn't realize the sacrifice you were making. What you were giving up by helping me out. We never talked about it then, and we don't have to talk about it now. Just know that you earned my gratitude and respect that day. Big time."

"Shit, Drake. I hate having talks like this."

"Fuck, you think I like them?" he asked. "Like I said, we don't have to say anything more."

I leaned closer to him and lowered my voice. "No, man. I

don't want you to go around thinking that I still have feelings like that for Lex. Or that I'm settling by dating Kaylie. 'Cause that's not the case at all."

"That's good to hear, because it was damn awkward being grateful to the guy who was in love with my girlfriend," he half-joked

"I'm sure that's an understatement. I honestly don't know how you were able to handle having me around Lex back then. If it were some guy friend of Kaylie's and I was in the same situation? I don't think I would have handled it as well as you did."

"It's not like I had much of a choice," Drake replied. "You guys had been friends for fucking ever. If I had told her she couldn't hang around with you anymore, she would have told me to fuck off. And it's not like she had any clue how you felt about her."

"That's the thing, man. My dad said something to me when I was home for Christmas break that didn't really hit me until I started dating Kaylie. Things with Lex were complicated. I was the one who introduced her to that douchebag. I was the one who partied with him our freshmen year here. Who walked into that room and found him cheating on her. And then had to tell her what happened. I felt so damn guilty about it all, and then when things went further to shit, I wanted to protect her so badly," I tried to explain.

"I get that, Jackson. And I appreciate that you were there for her back then."

I interrupted Drake before he could say anything else. "You're missing the point. I got so wrapped up in the situation, and it was the first time I realized how grown up she was. That she was hot. And with all those feelings hitting me for the first time, I figured I was in love with her," I admitted. Drake shifted in his seat, starting to look uncomfortable with where I was taking this conversation. "Chill out, man. I said 'I figured.' Not that I am in love with her. Because my dad was right. If I had really loved Lex like that, I would have done something about it. No way I would have waited two years, fucking around the whole time, and then stood on the sidelines and watched her fall for you without doing anything about it."

Drake heaved a deep sigh. "That's the part I never understood. Why you waited so long. But it's not like I could have asked you about it back then."

"Because I had it all fucked up in my head. And it took my relationship with Kaylie for me to realize how wrong I was back then. If the same situation happened with her, there's no way I'd be able to stand aside without fighting to make her mine."

"Damn, Jackson. You have no idea how much of a fucking relief it is to hear you say that," Drake admitted.

"Does that mean you aren't sitting over there thinking about how much you'd like to punch me in the face anymore?" I joked, relieved to have cleared the air with him since Lex would always be a part of my life and it didn't look like he was going anywhere anytime soon.

"Maybe not right now, but I'm sure you can still be a major pain in the ass. So don't rule it out for the future. Besides, you got to pop me one, so don't I still owe you?"

"Dude, you can't owe me a huge fucking favor and a punch to the face," I said, shaking my head.

"Sure I can," he replied before looking down at his phone, a big-ass grin spreading across his face. "Fuck."

"What?"

"Lex just sent me a few photos." He was scrolling through the messages he'd just received. "Looks like the girls are having a blast at The Rooster."

Fuck! I couldn't have just heard him right. "Hold up! Did you just say that the girls are at The Rooster tonight?"

"Yeah, dude."

"The Rooster? As in the campus bar where my girlfriend works?"

"Don't know of any other place that's got the same name, so that would be a yes. Kaylie told Aubrey that she should stop by sometime during one of her Thursday-night shifts, and they decided it would be perfect for their girls night because then they could include Kaylie and Char in their fun instead of it just being the two of them or some shit like that. Chill out, man. Why are you freaking out about this?"

Shit. Fuck. Damn. Not being able to hang out with your girl the day after you had sex for the first time wasn't good. Finding out that your sister and the girl you thought you had been in love with for two years were spending time with her instead? Well that was just bound to be a major clusterfuck of epic proportions.

CHAPTER 13

KAYLIE

"I'm so glad you told Aubrey to stop by so we could hang out while we're working," Char told me. "You were totally right when you said that she and I would get along really well. She's so fucking hilarious."

"Yeah, but I didn't know that she was going to bring Lex with her," I said, glancing down the bar at both of them. I didn't know Lex that well. She seemed nice enough, and I was trying not to act all weird. It was kind of awkward to be hanging out with her knowing that Jackson once had feelings for her. We hadn't really talked about it, and we hadn't even really defined our relationship. But after last night, I guess I was feeling a little sensitive about where things stood. This was horrible timing.

Char came closer so that she could whisper without anyone overhearing our conversation. "You know that Jackson is totally into you, right?"

"Yes," I replied before shooting a look Lex's way again.

"No, Kaylie. Like head-over-heels into you. I might not know the whole story, but I can see the wheels turning in your head tonight. Don't second-guess yourself or your relationship with Jackson. If you have questions about Lex, ask him."

"I know I am probably just being silly, but every once in a while I have that little voice in the back of my head that wonders if the only reason he's with me is because he can't be with her instead. But what if I don't like the answer?" I worried aloud.

"Then it's better that you know where you stand now before you get in any deeper. I've heard the same rumors as you about her being the reason he never dated and just did the whole one-night stand thing. But they are just rumors. And even if they are true, he sure didn't hesitate to throw that rule out the window for you. That's gotta mean something, Kaylie."

Char was right—as usual. I'd never actually heard Jackson say that he loved Lex. He hadn't really talked about her that much except when he was telling childhood stories or talking about stuff she did with his sister. And when he had mentioned her, he hadn't seemed any different than when we talked about anything else. Surely if there were something for me to worry about, then I'd have noticed it before now.

You could tell that Lex and Aubrey had known each other forever. It was hard to feel threatened by her when she had no problem making it completely obvious that she was totally in love with her boyfriend with the way she talked about him and kept sending him messages throughout the night. And when Aubrey introduced us, she'd seemed thrilled to meet me because she'd heard lots of great things about me and excited that Jackson was dating someone. It was pretty damn clear she had no interest in him as boyfriend material and acted like she was just his other sister. But that still didn't stop the questions from popping into my head as the evening wore on.

I walked over to where Aubrey and Lex were sitting at the other end of the bar. "You girls ready for another round?

"Hmmm," Aubrey said as she thought about. "Sure! Bartender's choice, but make it a crazy one this time around."

Lex giggled in response to Aubrey's request. "Yeah, pick something dirty. Gimme something good to text Drake and drive him a little more crazy."

"Dirty I can do," I assured them as I mixed their next round. I poured in a shot each of spiced rum and coconut rum with peach schnapps and pineapple juice. "Okay, spread 'em," I said, sliding their drinks in front of them.

"Spread what?" Aubrey asked.

"Your legs. That's what this drink is supposed to get you to do. It's called A Leg Spreader," I explained.

"Oh, I'm sure I will be spreading my legs tonight," Lex joked as she tossed the drink back. "No help needed from a drink for that to happen."

"Damn, I haven't spread my legs in so long that I don't know if I even remember how," Aubrey complained before drinking hers.

I blushed, thinking that I could have said the same thing before my time with her brother last night. But there was no way in hell I was going to say that. Way too awkward.

"Bit of a dry spell?" Char asked as she came up behind me.

"She gets tons of offers," Lex threw in.

"Yeah, it's a self-imposed one," Aubrey explained. "But that doesn't mean that I don't miss it."

"I totally get that," Char said. "With me here and Shane back home, my vibrator gets a major workout in the time between when we get to see each other."

"Ohmigod, I so know what you mean!" Aubrey agreed.

"She's not joking," I said dryly. "I've thought about buying stock in LELO with how much Char raves about hers. I'm just surprised that Shane isn't jealous of how attached she is to her vibrator."

"Nah. He knows that, as much as I enjoy the hell out of it when he's not here, it's still only a substitute for the real thing. And besides, he likes to see how crazy he can make me with it sometimes, too."

"Jesus, Char. TMI!" I shrieked, looking at Lex and Aubrey, who didn't really know her well enough to understand that she didn't have the same boundaries as other people. "Geesh, maybe you could share a little less with the new people?"

"No way," Lex interjected. "She's giving me ideas to use for later."

"Yeah! She can be our sexpert," Aubrey offered. "For, you know, when I decide to have sex again or something."

We all busted up laughing as we glanced around to make sure nobody was paying much attention to us with all the sex talk. Luckily, Thursday nights weren't too busy. Char and I still worked them because there were enough customers to make decent tips, but it usually died down earlier than Friday or Saturdays, so we pretty much had the place to ourselves right now except for a handful of tables, the waiter, and our boss, who was hiding out in back doing God knows what.

"You know, taking a break from the dating scene was a good idea, right?" Lex asked Aubrey.

"I do. It's just nights like these when I'm feeling a little frisky that it gets hard to stick to my guns."

"Well, you can always change your mind. Or drink enough to get past the frisky stage and make it to the falling-down-drunk one instead," Char chimed in.

"I like the sound of the falling-down-drunk option," Aubrey replied. "Let's go that route. How about another round of drinks for my bestie and me?"

"I think I'll pass this time," Lex said. "Someone has to be ready to hold your hair back if you're going that route. Plus, I don't want to rule out the possibility of sex tonight by getting so drunk that I pass out."

"Damn. I don't want to drink alone," Aubrey complained.

"I don't think that will be a problem," I said as I watched Jackson walk into the bar with Drake at his side. "For either of you, since your boyfriend just showed up, Lex. And I'm pretty sure we can convince your brother to have a lemon drop shot with you, Aubrey."

I smiled at Jackson and poured two shots as they approached us, getting a third ready to go in case Drake was interested in having one also. Jackson had a worried look on his face as he watched me the entire time. I gave him a questioning look, trying to figure out what was bothering him. Maybe he hadn't had fun on his guys' night and that was why they were here instead of out doing something.

I had the drinks ready when they made it to the bar. "You guys have perfect timing. I'm working hard to get Aubrey trashed and Lex just bailed on the drinking portion of tonight's entertainment. Which one of you will do a shot with her instead?"

Jackson glanced at Aubrey and shook his head when he realized she was already well on her way to drunk. He flashed a quick grin at Lex and then Char before turning his attention back to me. His grin turned into a full-out smile when I gestured at the shot glasses and nodded my head in his sister's direction, trying to hint that he should have one with her.

"Sure. I think I can handle a shot with my sis. Not sure she can handle another one though," he teased her.

"Hey, I've got a head start on you is all," Aubrey answered.

"You wouldn't believe the crazy-ass drinks your girlfriend has been serving me all night. We started out pretty tame with some Sex on the Beach but she made us Leg Spreaders the last time around. You better watch out for her, Jackson. She's a naughty one."

"Naughty, huh," he murmured under his breath, his gaze heating up. I'd bet just about anything that he was thinking about last night.

"Oh, stop eye-fucking her already and take the shot," Char taunted him. "You guys are bound to melt my panties off if you keep that up, and I'm wearing my favorite pair!"

"Hurry up and take the shots," I pleaded with them. "Before my roommate says something inappropriate. Oh, wait! Sorry. She already did."

Char punched me lightly in the shoulder before walking away to start breaking down for the night. We'd already announced last call, and she wanted to get a jump on cleaning tonight so she wouldn't feel guilty leaving it all for me while she raced home to have some sexy Skype time with Shane tonight. With Jackson here, she could even take my car instead of riding back with the girls.

"Hey, Jackson?" I asked to get his attention. "Do you think you could wait around and give me a ride back to campus?"

"Oh, he'll give you a ride alright," Aubrey slurred. It looked like that last shot had been enough to push her well past her limit.

I laughed at her joke, thinking that it would be great if she were right even though I was still a little sore from the last ride he gave me before pouring her a glass of ice water and pushing it across the bar to her.

"I think you're going to need this."

Jackson picked up the water and handed it to his sister with a stern look before glancing at Drake, who nodded his head. "Of course I can. Drake can go back with the girls and make sure Lex doesn't have a problem getting my sister into bed safely. What about your car?"

"That's where I come in," Char announced, walking back up to us. "Kaylie's trying to make sure I get plenty of time on Skype with Shane before she makes it back to the dorm. So please, take as long as you'd like to bring her back. Maybe even all night again."

"Char!" I gasped as I felt a blush creep up my neck and face since she'd basically just announced to the group that Jackson and I had had sex last night.

"Crap! Sorry, Kaylie," she apologized.

"Oh, please. Like everyone doesn't know you guys are having sex with the way my brother looks at Kaylie," Aubrey said.

"Okay, that's enough out of everyone," Jackson warned as he leveled the group with a glare. "End of subject."

"How about I get you two back to your dorm, baby?" Drake asked as he looked down at Lex, who was standing in the crook of his arm, beaming up at him.

"Thanks. I can definitely use the help," she replied before turning to look at me. "I'm really glad you asked Aubrey to come out. This was a ton of fun. It was nice getting to know you a little bit. I can see why Jackson's finally dating since he met you."

She really was very sweet, which kind of made me feel like a bitch for wanting to punch her in the face when I first saw her with Aubrey tonight. Luckily, I had been super nice to cover for being uncomfortable around her at the start of the night so she'd had no clue what was going on in my head at the time. Only Char had noticed because she knows me too well.

"Yeah, I'm glad you both could make it. We'll definitely have to do it again sometime. Maybe even on a night when Char and I aren't working so we can all go out and have some fun."

"Definitely," Aubrey giggled as Drake and Lex bundled her up and out the door.

"Do you mind waiting while I finish breaking down the bar and cleaning up?" I asked Jackson.

"Not at all, sweetheart. I never mind waiting for you."

He could be so damn sweet sometimes. "It should only be another thirty minutes or so. I'll give Char my keys so she can head out and meet you out front when I'm done?"

"Sounds like a plan. I'll pull the truck up and wait until you're done."

I watched his ass when he walked away and couldn't help but wonder if I had left any marks when I dug my nails in it last night. I shook my head to clear my thoughts as the rest of the customers left the bar and the waiter started to wipe down the tables so he could bail as soon as possible. I needed to get my butt in gear so I could spend some time with Jackson before he dropped me off. I still wanted to know what the deal was with the concerned expression he'd had when he came in tonight.

****

I found Jackson in his truck parked out front just like he'd said I would. I climbed inside the passenger's side door and leaned over to give him a quick kiss hello since I hadn't been able to do it earlier when I was working.

"I missed you today," I admitted as he pulled me across the cab and into his lap when I tried to pull away after my kiss.

"Fuck, I missed the shit out of you too, Kaylie. I couldn't get you out of my head all day," he replied before crashing his lips against mine. His kiss was quick, but he kept me wrapped in his arms when he was done so that he could peer into my eyes.

"I hope you didn't have to try too hard or have a reason to want me out of your head."

"No, I really didn't," he responded.

"Jackson, what's wrong?" I asked, a little worried by how serious he seemed.

"I was worried about you."

"You were?" I was surprised by his response. Sure, we hadn't seen each other since this morning, but last night had been awesome and everything had seemed okay when he dropped me off at my dorm this morning.

"Yeah. I didn't realize the girls were going to drop by the bar tonight."

"I didn't either, but I'd suggested it to your sister a while back because I thought she and Char would really hit it off," I explained.

"It was nice of you to invite Aubrey out, but I wasn't sure how you'd feel about Lex tagging along with her tonight."

And there it was—time for a difficult conversation. I pulled away from him and moved across the cab of the truck to my seat.

"Yeah, that was a shocker to me, too. And I can't say it was a nice one at first because it was pretty awkward for me. Could we maybe go somewhere to talk instead of doing this here in the parking lot?"

Jackson heaved a deep sigh and nodded his head. "Of course we can."

We were both silent during the drive back to campus. Jackson headed straight to the frat house once we got there and parked on the street. He hopped out and came over to open my door for me. Now I was starting to freak out a little because he still had the same worried look on his face. I reached for his hand to squeeze it, needing a little reassurance as we entered the house and went straight up to his room.

I kicked off my shoes, took my coat off, and sat down cross-legged on the end of his bed. Jackson closed and locked the door before he joined me on the bed. He looked down at his hands as I waited for him to say something, anything. My heart dropped to my stomach, fearing that this was going to be really bad. The thought of going from the best night of my relationship with him to possibly the worst within twenty-four hours was a little terrifying.

Jackson finally looked up and started to talk. "I know you've heard stuff about my feelings for Lex. Hell, you were there when Sasha accused me of avoiding relationships because I was in love with her. Yet in all the time we've been dating, you haven't asked me about it."

Since he paused, I took the opportunity to explain. "At first I wondered a little. I'd heard the rumors on campus, and of course I heard everything Sasha had to say when you were fighting. And I was a bit concerned since it seemed pretty damning that you stopped sleeping around when Lex got serious with Drake. But I guess at first I wasn't sure what exactly was going to happen with us so I didn't say anything."

"But it is something that's been bothering you?"

"I wouldn't say *bother* exactly. Yeah, it's crossed my mind from time to time, but there's nothing you've done since we've been together to make me think you're pining over her or anything like that," I answered.

"Fuck. The last thing I want to do is have to explain this to you because it's so damn embarrassing, but you need to know that's not what's going on here."

"Embarrassing?" I asked, not understanding but relieved to hear that this wasn't going to be the horrible news I'd thought it might be on the way over.

He ran his fingers through his hair in a frustrated gesture. "Some shit went down in her life, and I felt responsible in a way. Things got all confused in my head, and I thought I loved her."

I didn't know what to think. His explanation wasn't making things any clearer, and it sure wasn't comforting to hear that he used to think he was in love with Lex.

"How can you be wrong about something like that?"

"If you'd asked me that question a couple months ago, I'd have told you there was no fucking way I was wrong about being in love with Lex. Then I watched her fall for Drake, and it stung a bit, but I just wanted her to be happy. During Christmas break, my dad pointed out that, as much as they love Lex, he didn't think we'd end up together. At first I was pissed, but then he pointed out a few things that make more sense now that I met you. I'm not the world's most patient guy, right?"

"I don't know. You've been pretty patient with me, Jackson."

He huffed out a little laugh at that. "Kaylie, I asked you out to dinner pretty much right away and wouldn't take no for an answer. I didn't wait long to kiss you or warn other guys off you. Maybe I was able to hold out a little while before we had sex, but it sure as shit wasn't without making any moves on you, and I thought about it constantly."

"I guess when you put it that way you weren't super patient, but you certainly didn't pressure me."

He pulled my hands into his as he continued with his explanation. "But I took action. And with Lex, I never did. No dates. No kisses. No intimate texts or phone calls. No stepping in and trying to win her for myself when Drake came on the scene."

"So you were just friends the whole time?"

"Yes, and because we were just friends, I felt like it was okay to fuck around. A lot," he stressed.

"Saying *a lot* might be an understatement if the rumors are all true."

He looked at me sheepishly before nodding his head. "Maybe that's true, but here's the thing that I never realized until after you and I started dating. If I really was in love with Lex, then I would have done something about it. Because there's no way I'd just let some guy come in and take you away from me. And if I was that into her, I wouldn't have messed around with other girls the way I did all that time. I wouldn't have really noticed them because I'd have been too wrapped up in her to see random chicks that way. Like I am with you."

"With me?"

"Yes, Kaylie. With you," he repeated.

"So what are you saying exactly?" I asked.

"I'm saying that you knocked me on my ass, opened my eyes, and made me realize how wrong I had been. With you, I threw all the rules out the window and didn't look back because there was just no damn way I wasn't going to date you."

"And how's that working out for you so far?"

"That depends. Are you pissed at me because of tonight?" he asked.

"No, Jackson. It was a little weird and uncomfortable, but I liked Lex. And I'm relieved to know that you're not only spending time with me because she isn't available," I said, admitting the concern that had been really bugging me, because I would have been crushed to know that I was just a substitute.

"Hell no, Kaylie. It fucking tears me up inside at the idea that you might have been feeling like that all this time. I'm with you because there isn't anyone else I want to spend time with more than you," he reassured me.

"That's a lucky coincidence since I feel the same way about you."

"Yeah, lucky is a fucking understatement," he said.

I crawled closer to him and straddled his lap, wrapping my legs around his waist. "I like being lucky."

"You know what I like? I'm not sure if you noticed that Aubrey called you my girlfriend tonight," he pointed out. "But I damn well did, and I liked the sound of it."

"Does that mean I get to call you my boyfriend?"

"Fuck yeah. Say it again," he growled, the mood in the room shifting.

"Jackson Silver is my boyfriend," I said huskily before I leaned down to kiss him on the lips.

That's all it took for him to take over. His kiss was so hungry, like he couldn't get enough of me. I could feel his cock hard underneath me, and I started rocking back and forth slowly, craving friction. Jackson lifted me a little so that I was sitting up on my knees and he unzipped my jeans. He slipped his hand inside and rested his fingers on the outside of my panties, just holding them there. I could feel the heat pouring from his skin, making me so wet.

I wiggled a little to try to get him to move his hand, but he reached out with the other one to grip my hip and hold me in place. When I stilled, he started to slide my jeans down my legs and nudged me up so he could get them off. Once done, he moved me back onto my knees and slid his hands up the insides of my thighs toward my pussy. He pulled my panties aside and quickly thrust a finger inside me. I moaned as he slowly slid it back out and in over and over again. He added another finger, stretching me more. He fingered me with teasing thrusts, removing them and circling my pussy but never touching my clit before sliding them back inside.

"Look at my girlfriend," Jackson said. "So fucking wet for me."

He gently pushed against my chest so that I lay back on the bed, his fingers still inside me.

"Please, Jackson," I moaned as I tightened my legs to create more friction.

Jackson bent his head and gently kissed my clit. The contrast of his soft tongue and his fingers' hard thrusts made me shudder. Then he licked my slit slowly and pushed his tongue inside the next time he removed his fingers. I took a deep breath when he started to rotate between fingering me, nipping at my clit, and slowly licking down my slit and inside. I clenched my eyes shut, desperate to climax. I was so close and just needed a little something more. Jackson gave it to me on the next thrust of his fingers when he shoved three inside and sucked my clit in his mouth at the same time, sending me over the edge.

"That's what I've wanted to see all day long. The look on your face as I am bringing you pleasure. I fucking love that I can drive you crazy," he murmured as he wiped his mouth on his arm. "It's so hot to watch."

"So are you," I whispered as I climbed onto my knees and pushed on his chest. I took a moment to admire him lying there before going after his zipper so that I could get him naked. "Take off your shirt for me," I said while I was tugging his jeans down his legs along with his boxers. I needed him naked so that I could get a taste of him. I hadn't really gotten the chance to explore his body last night, and I wanted my turn now.

I kissed his chest and flicked his nipples with my tongue before I moved farther down his ripped abdomen. I trailed my tongue along his six-pack as I ran my fingernails up his thighs, stopping to dig them into his skin a few times because his hips jumped each time I did it. It didn't take long for me to reach his cock, and I licked the tip to taste the pre-cum that had been glistening there.

"Mmmmm," I hummed as I sucked him into my mouth.

"Yes, sweetheart. Just like that," he murmured before gripping my hair in his hands and holding me in place so he could thrust into my mouth. "Such a good girl, sucking me deep just like I've thought about you doing."

I flicked my tongue over the tip of his cock each time he pulled out and swirled it around when he pushed back inside. With each thrust, he went a little deeper into my mouth. He'd taken control of my blowjob, basically fucking my face now, and I loved it. I wanted to see him as I pushed him over the edge, and I could tell he was getting closer and closer each time he left my mouth and I tasted more pre-cum. I started to play with his balls, rolling them in my hand and gently squeezing. His eyes popped open and burned brightly on me as he watched his cock, slick with my saliva, moving in and out of my mouth.

At the next thrust, I sucked as hard as I could, not wanting to let go. Instead of pulling out, he pumped his hips in small bursts a few times before warning me. "I'm gonna come, sweetheart."

He let go of my hair, giving me a chance to pull away. I didn't though. I sucked him as deep into my mouth as I could get him before he started to go off. I felt him ejaculate deep into my throat and waited for him to finish before pulling back to swallow. He was staring at me with a satisfied look on his face when I licked my lips.

"Mmmmm. Turnabout is fair play."

Jackson pulled me down so that I was lying on top of him. "Stay the night."

"I really wish I could, but I should go back to the dorm at some point."

"I'll make it worth your while," he offered.

"I'm sure you would, but that doesn't change what I need to do. And if I stay with you, we're going to have sex again, but I need a little recovery time. I can still feel you inside."

Jackson looked at me with concern. "Damn, did I hurt you?"

"No, I'm not in pain exactly. It's just a little uncomfortable because it's been a while for me."

"Fuck, I should have made you take a bath at the cabin. It would have helped, and I can't do that for you here."

"Jackson, really. I'm fine. I promise," I murmured.

We lay there together for a little while until I felt myself starting to drift asleep. I jerked awake, and Jackson must have felt the movement.

"I guess I'd better get you back unless I can talk you into staying."

He looked so comfortable, and it felt good to rest in his arms. So I relented. "I guess it would be okay if you just take me back early in the morning."

CHAPTER 14

JACKSON

Waking up with Kaylie in my bed quickly became an addiction I had no intention of kicking. There wasn't a week that went by over the next few months where we didn't sleep together most of the time. It got to the point where I couldn't sleep as well when she wasn't with me since I was so used to holding her in my arms. For a guy who used to be known for kicking girls out the minute the fun was over, I'd sure as shit gotten used to the boyfriend role pretty damn quickly. It was ironic how little effort it had taken on Kaylie's part to hook me so completely.

It seemed like people on campus had finally gotten used to Kaylie and me as a couple. The guys at my frat took to her being around right away—not that I would have paid any attention if they'd had a problem with her. They did rib the shit out of me for being pussy-whipped all the time though. And my sister was fucking thrilled that I was with Kaylie. She probably would have been happy that I was dating just about anyone, but she was over the moon that I'd ended up with someone she liked. They'd gotten closer, and it was nice to see the women in my life getting along so well. I loved my sister, but she could be hell on wheels sometimes, and there was always the chance that she would have made things difficult if she'd hated the girl I was dating. Instead, I figured she'd give me hell at this point if I fucked things up with Kaylie.

The girls on campus were the last to come around to the idea of me being in a relationship. I found it fucking hilarious that they'd had no problem hopping in my bed with the hope that I might decide I wanted them around for more. But the second I met a girl I really did want to keep around? Well, that shit apparently didn't fly and the claws started to come out. I made it crystal clear that any chick who messed with Kaylie was on my shit list, so that didn't last very long. But the catty glares didn't stop. And it took for-fucking-ever for the sexual offers and heavy flirting to finally come to an end. I had to shoot down girl after girl any time Kaylie wasn't with me before they finally clued in that I wasn't interested. Hell, I even had to turn down some offers while I was with Kaylie from rude-as-shit women who seriously thought I'd be okay with them disrespecting my girlfriend like that.

Kaylie never complained about it though. Either she was the least insecure woman ever or she just didn't care enough to worry if I'd stray. And I was too much of a chickenshit to ask her which one it was because I wasn't sure I would like the answer. She never talked about what would happen with us after graduation and always changed the subject when I brought it up. It was tough as shit to get her to really open up about anything. Our lives had been so different, and I tried to be patient since I understood that the future was something she tried to not think about since she didn't really trust in it after what had happened to her parents. But it was so fucking hard because I wasn't a patient person, and I could see myself with Kaylie long term.

A future of having Kaylie in my bed night after night was something I could so easily picture in my head. I knew it should freak me out, but things were so good with her that it didn't. And it certainly didn't hurt that the sex between us just kept getting better and better. I wouldn't have thought it was possible, but as we learned each other's bodies, we figured out exactly what the other person liked. We both used it to our advantage so we could drive each other wild, almost like it was a contest to see who could do a better job of making the other lose control. I still fantasized about tying her up so she was at my mercy, but I hadn't brought it up again—yet. I figured I could afford to be patient because I fully intended to make sure it happened. I had plenty of time since there was no way I was letting her get away.

Kaylie was going to be busy all day getting ready for her dance thing tonight, so I was on my way to meet Aubrey for lunch. We hadn't hung out just the two of us in a while, and I was looking forward to catching up with what was going on in her world. I hadn't seen her out as much lately, and I wasn't sure if it was because I'd been so busy with Kaylie or if there was something going on with her that I needed to know about. I didn't talk to Lex as much anymore either, but I still knew that she would have called me if she'd thought Aubrey needed my help, so I hadn't worried about it too much. It hadn't been until Kaylie asked me if she was okay that I'd realized that she'd definitely seemed more than a little off lately. I hadn't seen her with any guys hanging around, so I couldn't help but wonder if some guy was about to get his ass kicked for breaking my little sister's heart.

When I pulled into the parking lot of her favorite local deli, I was surprised to see she was already there since Aubrey was notorious in our family for being late, and it usually wasn't even just a little bit late either. We all teased her about it, pointing out that she'd even been late for her own birth since my mom had gone a full week past her due date when my little sis was born. My brothers thought it was hilarious because all of us boys had been early, and my mom had been so pissed when she didn't have her a week early. To my mom, it was like Aubrey had been two weeks late instead, and she still complained about it any time one of us brought it up. Aubrey was so used to it by now that she just used it as her excuse whenever she was late for anything and passed the blame to Mom for not getting her out of there on time.

As I walked into the deli, I quickly scanned the room for Aubrey. She was already at a table with drinks and sandwiches in front of her. I glanced at my phone to check the time to make sure I hadn't totally messed up, but I wasn't running late so she must have gotten here early. Very strange. When she spotted me, a huge grin flashed across her face, settling my nerves a little bit.

"Hey, bro," she greeted me as I sat down. "I hope you don't mind. I took the liberty of grabbing your favorite stuff from here. I was starving so I didn't want to wait until you got here to order."

"Aubrey, when have you ever known me to be upset when there's food waiting to be eaten?"

"How about when Dad's the one who cooked it?" she teased, knowing damn well we all ran in the other direction the rare times that he decided to help Mom out by making dinner. He was a disaster in the kitchen.

"Well played," I said before taking a huge bite of the corned beef sandwich in front of me.

We both ate in silence until most of the food was gone. She

hadn't been joking when she said she was starving. Which meant something was wrong because Aubrey was a nervous eater. Any time something was worrying her, she went to food for comfort, thanks to our mom for having used it that way with us when we were younger.

"Mmmmm, that was so good," she said, wiping her mouth with her napkin.

"Okay, Aubrey. Spill."

"What do you mean?" she asked, trying to sound all innocent like she didn't know that I knew something was going on.

"You know exactly what I mean"' I responded as I pointed at the empty plates in front of us. "You know I appreciate you ordering lunch and all, but I know that when you eat like this something's bothering you. How can I help you if you don't talk to me about it?"

"Shit, Jackson. It's not me I'm worried about," she admitted.

That wasn't what I had expected her to say. "Then what the fuck is going on? Because you've seemed different lately."

"I'm fine, Jackson. I know I've changed a little over the last few months, but it's just because I'm finally growing up. And just in time because I'm going to be a senior soon. I can't act like a child my whole life."

"Aubrey, one of the things I love most about you is that you can still act like a kid sometimes. Don't change too much, okay? It's part of what makes you who you are. Although I am sure the parental units will be thrilled at the idea of you taking school and stuff more seriously."

"Yeah. I've even talked to Dad about working in one of the branches this summer," she surprised me with since she'd always been so against working for our dad.

"Whoa! Really? What made you decide that?"

"I think it's because I see so many people around me with purpose in their lives while I've been drifting a little aimlessly," she replied. "Lex has her planes. Drake has rugby. You have banking. Kaylie has dance. Hell, even Char has her parents' bar to go back to if that's what she decides she wants to do next. All I will have is a shiny degree that says I did my time here with no plan for what's next."

"So the bank is going to be your plan?"

"For now. Maybe I'll find something else, but it's as good a place as any to start. As long as you don't think I'm butting in or anything?" she asked. "We've always known you were the one of us kids who was going to end up working with Dad ever since you took to math so well and the rest of us kids didn't."

"Aubrey, I don't mind at all. I'd love it, and I am sure Dad will too," I reassured her. "But if that's not what's bothering you, then what is?"

The smile that had been plastered across her face from seconds ago wiped completely off. "It's Kaylie."

"Kaylie? Is something wrong?" I asked as I grabbed my phone to see if she'd tried calling me and I'd somehow missed it.

Aubrey reached out to stop me before I dialed Kaylie's number. "I didn't explain that very well. You know how she has the showcase tonight?"

"Yeah?" I asked, still not getting where she was going with this.

"Has she talked to you about it very much?"

"Not really. It's just a show for the end of the year, right? What is there that really needs to be said about that?" I asked, still not understanding.

"Shit, Jackson," she sighed. "There are going to be scouts from dance companies there. People who are going to be there in part because Kaylie is dancing."

"Okay, and your point is what, exactly?"

"I know she means a lot to you, Jackson. I can tell how much any time I'm around the two of you or even just when someone mentions her to you. Your whole face lights up. So my point is this. What are you going to do if she gets an offer to go dance somewhere like New York or Chicago or Los Angeles? Dancing has been her thing since she was a little girl, and it means even more to her now because it makes her feel close to her mom. Have you guys even talked about what comes next for you with graduation just around the corner?"

Fuck yeah, I had thought about what would come next for Kaylie and me, but I hadn't factored her getting her dream job offer that far away from home into the equation. "I guess if that happens then I have some serious thinking to do, Aubrey. Because I'm not ready for this thing to end between us even if she ends up a thousand miles away."

CHAPTER 15

KAYLIE

Time today flew by, and before I knew it, the showcase was about to begin. There had been a last-minute issue with my costume so I hadn't had time to go out front to make sure Jackson made it here okay and found his seat. This was the first time I'd danced in front of Jackson on stage, and I wanted him to enjoy it. Knowing that he would be in the audience cheering me on helped calm my nerves each time I thought about the fact that there would be others out there who were here to judge my every step. I learned this afternoon that my aunt would be here, so I already knew there would be at least one person out there who would find fault with my dancing. So I tried to focus my thoughts on dancing for Jackson and not worrying about what anyone else would think.

Jackson: Good luck tonite!
Kaylie: Thx :) C u soon.

I couldn't help but chuckle when I realized it was Jackson who'd just sent me a text. He had the most amazing sense of timing. It was almost like he had a sixth sense when it came to me, calling or texting when I was thinking about him. Although it might not be saying too much since I thought about him almost constantly, I couldn't count how many times I'd grabbed my phone to dial his number only to pick up a call from him instead. It was kind of eerie sometimes. Almost like we had some ESP thing going on between us. Which made it very difficult to keep things from him like I was with my dancing.

It hadn't started out that way on purpose. I hadn't realized that Jackson wouldn't know that I wanted to dance professionally. I mean, I was a dance major for a reason. But he wasn't really familiar with the dance world except from his sister's perspective. I really adored Aubrey, but dancing was just a hobby for her. So his perspective on dance was a little skewed by that. Not that dancing for fun wasn't awesome, because it was. I just wasn't ready to give up on my dream of dancing professionally yet.

I needed this dream to define me. It was what I'd held on to ever since my parents died. My mom was a huge dreamer, too. I hoped to be like her and never stop chasing my dreams. There's nothing more magical than when you catch one and hold it in your hand, even if just for a moment. And this was the performance that would determine the rest of my life as a dancer. If I was going to be able to catch this dream or not. And I hadn't been ready to share all of that with Jackson because I was scared to death that being so happy with him was going to make me rethink this dream when I wasn't ready to do that yet.

Talking to him about my hopes and fears would have just made them more real. So for once, I just went with the flow and pushed all my concerns aside to focus on today instead of worrying about what would happen tomorrow. It was only now that I thought about how that might make Jackson feel if I did get an offer and had to explain to him that I'd known there was a chance this would happen. And I felt like a total bitch for not talking to him sooner. I didn't know how I would be able to make this right or if I even could. Because now, if I did actually get an offer, it would affect him too. I couldn't pretend that it wouldn't any longer. The moment of truth was here, and it was entirely possible that I had let my fear of being abandoned create a situation where Jackson would have every right to walk away from me. And it would be my own damn fault.

But I couldn't focus on that right now. I needed to go out there and dance like I'd never danced before. Less than an hour of acting like an ostrich with its head in the sand and pretending that nothing could go wrong was totally doable. It had to be because the only alternative was failure. And with my aunt out there ready to tell me 'I told you so' about my decision to attend Blythe, I wasn't ready to admit defeat.

"Kaylie, you're on in ten minutes," one of the stage hands yelled to me across the dressing room.

I moved to do one more round of stretches, warming my muscles up so I'd be ready to go when it was my turn. As I stretched, I visualized the choreography in my mind, picturing myself moving through each step flawlessly. It was a trick one of my dance coaches had told me about years ago that worked really well for me.

Before long, they were announcing my name. I took one deep, cleansing breath to clear my head and moved towards the stage, waiting for the first beat of my music to begin. I heard my cue and moved onto the stage for what ended up being the fastest three and a half minutes of my life.

By the time it was over, I was panting heavily from the exertion with sweat dripping down my body. I felt like it had gone really well, that I had made it into the zone where I could do no wrong. As I walked off the stage, I was sure that, no matter what happened, I could be happy with the fact that I'd done my personal best and left everything I had inside me out on the dance floor. If I didn't get an offer, then at least I wouldn't have anything to regret about my performance.

Several people offered me their congratulations as I made my way back to the changing area. I nodded absently in response, focused on getting cleaned up so I could just go find Jackson. Now that it was over, I felt an urgent need to talk to him about everything going on in my head. I just hoped that I hadn't waited too long.

****

Once I had changed back into my street clothes and made it to the lobby to search for Jackson, the place was packed. I was one of the last performances of the night, and I'd had a ton of makeup on that I'd wanted to wash off. I'd thought I hadn't taken that long to get ready, but apparently it was still longer than everyone else based on the mob of people I had to weave my way around while I was searching for him. I finally spotted him across the room and was headed that way when I heard my aunt's voice from behind me.

"I certainly hope you don't expect to get a good offer after that performance, Kaylie," she said in her grating tone of voice.

Jackson's eyes were on me, so I gave him a reassuring smile before turning to great my aunt. "Hello, Kathy."

Her expression turned icy with my words. "How many times do I have to tell you not to call me that disrespectful name? You know that it's either Kathleen or Aunt Kathleen, Kaylie. Really, must you be so immature? You're getting ready to graduate from college. I would have thought you'd have outgrown this kind of behavior by now."

Okay, maybe it was immature to always use a nickname I knew she hated. But I was okay with it because it got to her every single time. And I'd take my wins with her where and when I could. I was pretty sure that wasn't going to change regardless of how old I was.

I offered her an extremely insincere apology. "Sorry, Aunt Kathleen."

Apparently she either chose to ignore my sarcasm or didn't catch it. "That's much better. Now, I've made some calls to see if we can get you some extra training before you go out on any auditions this summer. I really wish you had taken my advice on gone to a school better suited to properly train you. You've developed some atrocious habits during your years here."

"That's funny because I thought I did very well tonight," I disagreed.

"Please, Kaylie. You know you've never been a good judge of that. Trust me when I say it will be an uphill battle to get anyone who was here to ever seriously consider you in the future. You have your work cut out for you if you want to undo the damage you've already done."

Jackson joined us in the middle of my aunt's tirade, placing his hand on my back in a comforting gesture. When he didn't walk past and continued to stand behind me, my aunt gave me a questioning look.

I introduced them. "Aunt Kathleen, this is my boyfriend Jackson. Jackson, this is my aunt."

Jackson stretched out his free hand to shake hers. "A pleasure, ma'am."

"It's nice to see Kaylie dating someone with manners," my aunt replied. "But I hope you understand that we are having a private conversation right now regarding her future. Would you mind waiting over there?" she asked as she gestured away from where we were standing.

I was mortified by her behavior. Jackson was being perfectly polite to her and she still had to be a major bitch just so she could continue to tell me what a horrible dancer I had become.

"Jackson, no. You don't have to go anywhere."

He leaned down to kiss my cheek before addressing my aunt. "Actually, I do mind waiting over there. Kaylie invited me to be here with her tonight, so that's exactly what I'm going to do."

"Well," Aunt Kathleen muttered. "I guess our conversation will just have to wait until tomorrow then since you are too busy with your boyfriend to have a serious discussion with me. Kaylie, plan on my picking you up for breakfast at your dorm at seven a.m."

I didn't even have the chance to respond and tell her that I didn't want to talk with her about this—let alone sit down for a meal—before Jackson jumped back into the conversation. "If your plan is to spend the whole meal talking down to Kaylie and badgering her, then I don't think she has time for you tomorrow morning either."

"Well, I don't recall asking you for your opinion," she snapped back at him.

"That's the great thing about being her boyfriend. You don't have to ask. It's my privilege to protect her from harm, and that includes you if necessary."

My aunt chose to ignore his comment. "Kaylie, I will be at your dorm in the morning, and I expect you to be ready when I get there."

I took a step closer to Jackson, gathering strength from his presence at my side. "Here's the thing, Kathy. You can show up at my dorm as early or late as you want tomorrow morning. It won't do you any good because I won't even be there. I'll be over at Jackson's place instead. So if you really want to spend time with me, then you can pick me up from there and invite him to come along with us."

"But be prepared to be nice to Kaylie or it's not going to be a pleasant meal," Jackson warned.

"If that's going to be your attitude, then I guess I'll just go back home earlier than planned. But I have to tell you that I am even more disappointed in you than I was when I watched you dance earlier, Kaylie. Not only have you wasted your talent by going here, but it appears that you've decided to follow in your mother's footsteps and allow a man to dictate your future," she shot back at me before marching away.

I watched my aunt disappear into the crowd with mixed feelings. I was happy that I'd stood up to her again. I was angry that she'd given me yet another reason to need to be firm with her in the first place. And I was sad because it felt so final, like this was the end of our relationship. Even though it was a strained one, she was still family and I hated to think that we'd never be able to get past our issues and be close to each other. I missed having family in my life, but I didn't think that my relationship with her was salvageable.

"You okay, baby?" Jackson murmured in my ear, sounding worried.

"Not really, but it's not like there's anything I can do about it to make things better unless I want to totally cave and do everything she says exactly when she wants me to do it. And I just can't do that."

"I'm sorry I didn't really make the situation any better. I think I made it worse," he apologized.

"No, Jackson," I reassured him. "That was all her. It really wasn't about you. If you hadn't been here, my conversation with her wouldn't have gone much better. In fact, I was happy that you were here to take my back. I liked how we felt like a team. I've never had that before, and it's kinda awesome."

Jackson smirked at me. "A team, huh?"

"Yeah, definitely."

He tilted his head like he was considering the idea. "I like the sound of that."

"And teammates share stuff with each other—even the hard stuff. Right?"

His teasing expression immediately sobered. "Yes, Kaylie. Sharing is important if we're going to be a team."

Shit. I was totally busted. He already knew something was going on, so I must not have been as good at hiding it as I'd thought I'd been. "When we're done here, we need to go somewhere to talk," I uttered the dreaded words no guy ever wants to hear.

Jackson didn't look too worried though. "I will always have time for you, sweetheart. If you ever have anything you want to talk about, I'm yours. Got it?"

I loved the sound of that, and I could tell that he wasn't joking either. He really meant it, and he'd never done anything in the time we'd been dating to make me think otherwise. That was going to make our conversation even more difficult since he was an open book to me while I'd been less open with him. If our roles were reversed, I would be pissed. And my feelings would be hurt. Knowing that I might have made Jackson feel bad or doubt how I feel about him was not a good feeling at all, especially with how much care he'd taken with my feelings.

I glanced around the lobby and watched all my classmates chatting, looking excited. Between my aunt and my upcoming talk with Jackson, the evening had lost some of its luster for me already. There wasn't anything keeping me here right now, so why wait any longer?

"I'm yours too, Jackson. So why don't we just get out of here now?"

"Don't you have people you need to talk to here before we leave?"

He made a good point. There was one person I needed to check in with before we could go. "Let's just stop to say goodbye to my mentor, and then we can head out."

We held hands as we walked through the crowded room over to my teacher. She was surrounded by a circle of people, so I waited until I could get her attention. She beamed a smile at me as soon as she noticed us standing there.

"Kaylie! I am so glad you found me," she greeted me before pulling me into her group, Jackson following behind me since I didn't let go of him.

"This is the dancer I was just telling you about. Kaylie Rhodes." She introduced me to several of the people with whom she had been speaking before we'd arrived. "And Kaylie, there are a couple people here who are going to want to talk to you about your plans for after graduation."

I was blown away when a couple of the women with her nodded their heads and smiled at me before introducing themselves. "You danced beautifully tonight," one of them said. "I'd be very interested in talking to you if you'd like to give me a call." Then she handed me her business card.

That conversation was repeated a few times. By the time Jackson and I left, I had four business cards held tight in my hand. Four different opportunities to dance professionally and make my dream come true. I could hardly believe it. I wanted to jump up and down and do a victory dance, but that hardly seemed appropriate right here in front of everyone. Besides which, my celebration might be too soon without knowing how the rest of my night would go now that the cat was out of the bag since Jackson had been right there with me as it all happened. And he'd been very quiet through it all, just giving my hand a quick squeeze here and there.

"Kaylie!" Char screamed as she came running towards me, interrupting my line of thought. She threw her arms around me for a big hug before stepping back. "Ohmigawd, you were amazing up there! So beautiful I could hardly believe that was you. Not that I didn't already think you were amazing. But tonight you took it to a whole new level!"

I held up the business cards for her to see. "Yeah, well. It looks like you weren't alone in thinking that."

She shrieked as she grabbed the cards from my hand to look through them—something I hadn't brought myself to do yet because I was too focused on Jackson right now.

"Holy fuck, Kaylie. This is some pretty amazing shit right here. Please tell me your aunt was here when this happened and you got to rub it in her sour face."

"No such luck. Jackson and I had already run her off before the good news."

Char glanced at Jackson standing next to me and back to me again. She knew damn well that I hadn't talked to him about what might happen tonight, and she gave me a worried look before greeting him.

"Hey, Jackson. Don't you think our girl was amazing tonight?"

"Yes, my Kaylie was fan-fucking-tastic."

She nodded her head, like that was exactly the answer she'd been looking for. "It looked like you two lovebirds were on your way out when I interrupted. I take it I won't get Kaylie back until the morning?" she asked Jackson.

"Yeah, I'm pretty sure that's a safe bet to take."

I was so relieved at his reply. He already knew that I might take a job dancing somewhere, but he still planned on being with me tonight. That tight feeling in my chest, the fear that I'd fucked up so badly I wasn't going to be able to fix it, loosened slightly.

"I'll see you tomorrow, okay?" I told Char as I gave her a quick hug.

"I'm so proud of you," she whispered, slipping the cards back into my hand before taking a step back.

"Love you," I mouthed to her as we walked away.

I'd walked to the auditorium, another one of my rituals before a big performance. It was convenient tonight because it meant I could ride with Jackson without having to worry about my car. The atmosphere in his truck was tense though, and my nerves started to come back when I realized he were headed to his parents' cabin. It wasn't an unusual thing for us to do, but it pretty much meant that this was going to be a conversation for which he wanted us to have privacy.

When we got there and made it inside, I used one of the oversized chairs instead of the couch where Jackson sat down. He gave me a strange look before shaking his head at my choice of seats and scooting down the couch so he was closer to me.

"I think you left out some details about your showcase tonight," he started, pausing so I could explain.

"I know, and I am so sorry. I would totally understand if you're completely pissed at me."

He shook his head in response. "Kaylie," he sighed. "I'm not mad exactly. Disappointed? Yes. Worried that you felt like you couldn't talk to me about shit like this? Yes."

"No, Jackson! It wasn't that I felt like I couldn't talk to you. I know that I can and you'll always listen. I'm not sure how to explain it though."

He ran a hand through his hair in a frustrated gesture. "Just tell me what you're thinking. What's going on in that mind of yours?"

"You know how much I love to dance," I began. He nodded his head because this was something we had discussed before. "The showcase was my best opportunity at a chance to dance professionally after school."

"So the people your dance teacher introduced you to tonight—they could offer you a job?"

"Yes," I sighed as I reached into my pocket to pull out their business cards. "This is huge. I had hoped that someone might possibly be interested, but this is more than I even let myself dream."

"Where are they from?" he asked, gesturing at the cards.

I shuffled through them and was shocked at the variety. "Chicago. San Francisco. And two are from places in New York."

"They're all pretty far away," he pointed out.

My heart sank at the thought that we wouldn't be able to figure this out somehow. Dance was my dream, but Jackson had quickly become a huge part of my happiness. If keeping my dream meant losing him, I just didn't know what I was going to do.

"Yeah, unfortunately they are. There just aren't a whole lot of opportunities to dance around here. I swear to God, if there were I would be interested because you're here."

"And this is what you want to do? Go somewhere to dance?"

I thought about how to explain it so that he would

understand and moved to a kneeling position at his feet as I answered. "Yes, Jackson. It really is what I want to do. It's my dream, and if I don't chase it now, then I will lose my chance forever. I'm just not ready to let go of it yet."

Jackson pulled me onto his lap and wrapped his arms around me. "I think that's what bothers me the most, Kaylie. That you would honestly think that I'd want you to give up your dream for me. You should know me better than that. I want what's best for you. Always."

I breathed a huge sigh of relief. "Even if it means that I have to move a thousand miles away?"

"Yes, Kaylie. Even then. But I need to know right now. Do you also want our relationship? Because I can't do this thing alone."

"I absolutely want you in my life," I whispered against his lips before kissing him.

"You need to fucking learn to talk to me," he replied after our kiss ended. "I know it's hard. Hell, after meeting your aunt, I don't know how the hell you ended up so sweet. And I definitely get why you learned to keep shit to yourself living with her. But if you want this thing to work between us, it's something you need to work on with me. Especially if you're going to move a thousand miles away to dance."

"I know, and I swear I will do better. I don't want to lose you, and I know that if I can't figure out how to let you in more I might."

"That's all I needed to hear," he reassured me. "I didn't want to ruin your big night, but I needed to know that you're in this for the long haul with me. Because I'm in it with you, Kaylie."

"Even if it means a long-distance relationship?"

"Yes, sweetheart. Even then," he murmured. "I already broke all my other rules. Why not this one too?"

CHAPTER 16

JACKSON

It was like the flood gates had opened between us when Kaylie and I spent the whole night after her showcase talking. She finally started sharing more of what was going on inside her head with me. Thank fuck, because I'd felt like an idiot asking my girlfriend to talk to me. I was probably the only guy in the world that had to practically beg his girl to talk to him when most other guys avoided serious conversations like the plague. I couldn't help but wonder how the hell I'd gone from being the one-night-stand guy to being so serious about Kaylie that I wanted to know everything about her.

It was pretty damn scary to think about the importance she had in my life now. My feelings for her were just so fucking intense. She had the power to crush me, and I didn't think she even realized it. I'd waited a long time to let a girl into my life, and now that I had, I'd gone full fucking throttle straight from the gate. No pussyfooting around for me. And the plan I was currently considering sure as shit showed how much Kaylie had come to mean to me in the short time we had been together.

Kaylie had dreams that meant a lot to her. They seemed to be the last tangible thing tying her to her parents. She worked damn hard to make those dreams come true, and there was no way I could be a roadblock to them for her. I wanted her to have every fucking good thing she wanted in her life. When she'd told me about the offer the dance company in New York had made, her eyes were shining so fucking bright that it was impossible to miss how much she wanted to go. But she was still considering her other options and had talked about possibly going to Chicago because it was closer to me. She was happy about that option, but she was thrilled about the idea of going to New York.

I hated the idea that she might miss out because she was factoring me into her decision just as much as I loved that she was thinking about my place in her life while she was considering her options. So I needed to find a way for her to be able to take the New York offer without worrying about our future as a couple, and I thought I'd finally figured out just how to do it. But I needed to talk to my dad about it first because it would completely change our plans for me after graduation. I was on my way to his office to do that right now, and I was nervous as hell that he'd tell me I was fucking crazy. I just might be, but I still wanted his support anyway.

I headed straight to his office as soon as I made it to the bank. Dad's secretary waved me in since I had called ahead.

"Hey, Dad," I said as I walked in and spotted him sitting behind his desk, working on his computer.

He stood up to walk around his desk and gave me a quick hug. "Hey, Jackson. Your call was a nice surprise. I don't know how long it's been since you popped into the office to see me during the workday. Don't you have a class or something? Or are things already winding down with graduation just around the corner?"

"I needed to talk to you and wanted to do it here, away from home, so it could be just the two of us."

My dad cocked his head and considered me for a moment. "That sounds pretty serious. Everything okay? Anything I can do to help?"

That was so like him, offering to jump in and help me before he even knew what was going on. "Things are good, Dad. But I do need your help with something."

He moved to the conference table and pulled a couple chairs out. "Well, come on. Sit down and let me know what you need."

I swallowed the lump in my throat at the thought that Kaylie didn't have this kind of support system behind her. No matter what I did or where I went, I would always have my parents' backing. That knowledge just made my decision even easier.

"I know you've planned on me coming to work for you here this summer for just about forever, Dad," I started. "I hate to disappoint you, but I want to wait before doing that."

"What would you do instead?" he asked, waiting to pass judgment until he had more information.

"I'd like to try to get a job at one of the bigger banks in New York."

"New York? That's certainly a big change of plans when you've always talked about staying in town," he pointed out.

"I know it is, Dad. But it will give me some valuable experience. I'll learn a lot because I'll have to start from the bottom without any favoritism out there. And I can bring that knowledge back with me when I return."

"You could start at the bottom here if it's favoritism you're worried about," he offered.

I took a deep breath before delivering the part of the news I figured would shock him the most. "Here's the thing, Dad.

Kaylie got an offer to dance there, and I know she wants to accept it. But she's considering a different offer that would let her stay closer to me so it would be easier for us to see each other more often."

"Jackson," he sighed. "How did I know this was somehow connected to Kaylie?"

"Trust me, I know it sounds crazy that I want to move halfway across the country to be with my girlfriend, especially when we haven't been together that long. And I don't even know what she's going to say about this idea because I haven't talked to her yet. I wanted to make things right with you first."

"Why do you think this is the right decision for you?" he asked.

"I think she could be it for me, as girly as that sounds coming from me. She has come to mean a lot to me in the time we've been together. We might be able to survive a long-distance relationship, but what we have between us is so new that I'm just not ready to test it that way yet."

He nodded his head as I was explaining, as though he got what I was saying. "I understand why you might have those worries, but have you considered maybe trying it out at first instead of jumping into this decision? I'd hate to see you make a life decision out of fear."

"Yeah, but that's only part of why I think this is right. I also want to be there for Kaylie. This is a huge change for her, and she doesn't have anyone else to support her except her friends. They won't be in New York with her, but even if they were, I'd still want to be there for her. No, that's not strong enough to explain it. I feel like I need to be there for her."

"It means that much to you? Being able to support her from there instead of here?" he asked.

I stopped to think for a moment. This was the moment of

truth. No hiding from my feelings. If I was going to get him on my side, I needed to lay it all on the line. "Yes, Dad. It means everything to me. I think she needs me there with her instead of here. And that makes it pretty damn simple for me. If Kaylie needs me, then I am going to find a way to be there for her. Because that's what I was made to do. Make her world a better place."

At my words, my dad's face broke into a beaming smile. "Then that's what you'll do, son. All your mom and I want for you is happiness. That's what I was trying to tell you back over Christmastime. You needed to find someone who makes everything else seem less important because they mean everything to you, like your mom does for me. If you need to go to New York for now so she can dance, then we'll figure it out. I've still got some contacts there, so I'm sure we can find you a job. But you need to live your own life, son. Don't worry about your mom and me or the bank. We'll all be here waiting for you if or when you want to come back."

That right there was why my dad was still my fucking hero. He was one of the strongest men I knew, but he still had no problem letting us know how important we were to him in both actions and words.

"Thanks, Dad," I muttered, relieved that I'd managed to explain this to him in a way that he understood why I was changing my plans so drastically.

"Don't thank me yet, Jackson. We still have to explain this to your mom," he reminded me. "And it sounds like you need to have a serious conversation with Kaylie, too."

I wasn't too worried about my mom. If my dad was already on board with the plan, she'd come around eventually. But I wasn't sure how Kaylie would take my news. I hoped she'd be excited, but it wasn't something we'd talked about at all. She hadn't asked me to come with her. The idea was all my own, but I wasn't going to wait around to see if she was going to ask me to go with her, because if I waited too long, she might do something impulsive and accept the Chicago offer. It might be ballsy of me to barge into her new life, but I was going to do it anyway.

CHAPTER 17

KAYLIE

The decision for where to go after school ended was so damn difficult. This was a time when I should be thrilled that my dreams were coming true. Instead, I was so unsure of what to do because I knew that whatever I decided would impact Jackson almost as much as it did me. When we talked about it, he'd assured me that I needed to go with whatever was best for me and we would figure out our situation after. But how was I supposed to do that when I knew that I could take us down a path that meant the end of our relationship?

I hadn't been looking for a relationship, but I guessed these things happened when they were meant to instead of when it was convenient for us. This was probably one of the worst times in my life for me to be worried about a boyfriend, but it just didn't matter. Jackson was a part of my life, and I wanted to keep him there, which meant I was going to go with the decision that would let me have my dream and still give me the best chance to keep him in my life. I was going to accept the Chicago offer. It might not be what my heart was telling me to do when it came to my dancing, but it was definitely what I felt I should do because of Jackson.

It wasn't that I thought he wouldn't support my decision to go to New York. I knew that he would back me up no matter what I chose to do. But the extra distance and the frantic pace of New York City meant that I would get even less time to build our relationship. As solid as things felt between us right now, I had to remember that this was still relatively new and needed time to grow deeper—time spent together, not apart.

I planned to tell Jackson my decision tonight. We were going to spend the night at the cabin again, so it was perfect timing since we would have some extra privacy we wouldn't get if we were at his frat or my dorm. He had plans for most of the day, so I was just meeting him there. With the school year almost over, I went ahead and quit my job at the bar so I'd have extra time to make sure I was ready to go when the time came. I also wanted to have extra time to spend with Jackson so that I could save up some memories for when I left. I finally had some flexibility in my schedule with the showcase being over and not working anymore.

When I made it to the cabin, Jackson's truck was already parked in front and there was a flickering light coming from inside. I hurried in because I didn't want to waste a minute of the time I had remaining with him. When I stepped inside, I saw that he'd gone all out. Dinner was on the table, candles were lit, and Adele was playing in the background. Jackson had really shocked me with how romantic he could be sometimes. I hadn't expected it of him, but I loved that he was willing to show his sensitive side to me on occasion. He always made sure I knew how much I meant to him. He worked hard to ensure I had no reason to ever doubt my place by his side.

"Hey, sweetheart," he greeted, walking towards me so he could pick me up and twirl me around before giving me a quick hello kiss. "Damn, I missed you today."

"Jackson," I sighed. How the hell was I supposed to be okay with losing the chance to have this in my life every single day? I had always respected Char for how she handled herself being so far away from Shane these last four years, but I never really understood how difficult it had been for her until now. No volume of phone calls, text messages, or Skype calls could possibly make up for not being able to touch Jackson whenever I wanted. We could talk a thousand times a day and I still didn't think it would be enough.

"No sad faces tonight, Kaylie. I swear to you it will all work out," he promised, easily reading my thoughts on my face.

How I wished he could make everything okay, but I just didn't see how it was possible. It was either dance or seeing him every day, and I just couldn't say no to my dream when it came knocking on my door. I tried to shake off this melancholy feeling so that I could enjoy this time I had with him now instead of wasting it by being sad. I hugged him tight, swallowing down the sudden lump in my throat.

"I know it will, Jackson. No matter what," I agreed, stepping back to move to the table. Jackson pulled out my chair, helping me get settled before sitting down himself. I couldn't help but think that it was these little things I might miss the most.

"I hope you're in the mood for Japanese. I stopped off to grab some carryout on my way over and got your favorites," he said, dishing food onto my plate from the containers in the middle of the table. He'd gone to the restaurant he'd taken me to for our first date. It was so fucking sweet. He really was pulling out all the stops to make my last days here as special as possible.

"It looks wonderful," I replied, suddenly feeling famished as I realized I had skipped lunch today. I quickly dug into the meal, enjoying every bite.

We were both fairly quiet while we ate, a comfortable silence hanging between us. We just enjoyed our food and being together, knowing we'd have time to talk once we were done. I appreciated that we could be together like this without it being awkward.

Once we were both full, we quickly cleaned up the mess and moved to the living room to sit on the couch. I was looking forward to some cuddle time with him, just hanging out.

"There's something we need to talk about," he said in a serious tone of voice. My smile must have slipped a bit at his words because he sat down and pulled me onto his lap. "It's not anything bad, Kaylie. In fact, I hope that you think this is something really good."

I cocked my head, trying to think what he could possibly be talking about but coming up empty. "Okay," I replied cautiously. "You've got my full attention. And there's something I wanted to discuss with you tonight too."

He tightened his grip on me, almost like he was afraid I was about to bolt. "I know you've been struggling to decide between going to Chicago or New York. When we talked about the different offers, you looked so excited about the idea of dancing in New York. It's what you've always dreamed about, and I want you to go for it."

"But, Jackson, that would mean I'd be even farther away from you. And the demands on my time would be so much more if I danced there," I worried, not telling him anything I hadn't already shared before.

"Not if I come with you," he argued.

My heart stopped at his words as I literally lost my breath for a moment, positive that I must have heard him wrong. "Come with me?" I repeated.

"I know it sounds crazy, but just hear me out before you say anything," he pleaded with me. "This thing between us might be pretty new, but I know that you mean a lot to me and I don't want to risk losing you with the distance that would be between us. It's not that I don't believe in our relationship, because I do. But I don't think it's worth the gamble when I have too much to lose. You."

"Jackson," I whispered, incredibly touched by his words.

"Not done yet," he said as he touched a fingertip to my lips, stopping me from saying anything else. "And it's not a bad idea for work either. I already talked to my dad about it, and he's making some calls to put feelers out with banks where he knows people. I could learn a lot about the industry from working at a bigger bank and bring that knowledge back with me when I'm ready to come back home and work with him in the future."

"You talked to your dad already?" I gasped, stunned that he'd put so much thought into this plan before talking to me about it.

"Yeah, today," he replied.

"And he's really okay with this?"

"I know. I was pretty damn shocked that I was able to make him understand why I feel like this is the right decision. But I've got his support, and he's going to talk to my mom tonight. So I guess the only real question now is what you think about the idea."

I took a moment to really consider the idea of both of us living in New York. It was clear he'd put a lot of thought into this, and I didn't want him to think I wasn't taking it as seriously as he obviously had.

"Well—" I drew the moment out. "I think it would be pretty

damn fantastic to have you there with me, as long as this is really what you want to do for yourself—not just for me."

"I don't think I've ever been more sure of anything in my life, Kaylie."

"Hot damn!" I shrieked, jumping off his lap. "I'm going to dance in New York City, Jackson!"

He watched me with a wide smile stretched across his face, his eyes lit from the inside as I danced around the room to celebrate this moment. It was like a huge burden had been lifted from my shoulders.

"I take it that means you're okay with the idea?"

I ran across the room and tackled him on the couch. "Okay doesn't even begin to describe how I'm feeling right now. I feel like I could take on the whole fucking world right now and win. I get to live my dream with you by my side. Did you really think that I wasn't going to jump at the chance for that?"

He chuckled lightly. "I'll admit I was a little worried you might think it was over the top, even for me."

"Not at all! I can hardly wait. I get to spend my days dancing and my nights in bed with you. How awesome is that?" I asked before a thought crossed my mind. "I do get to spend my nights with you, right? I guess I kind of assumed that this meant you wanted to live together."

"Hell yes, that's what I'm saying, Kaylie."

"Woohoo! We're going to live in sin together, baby," I teased. "Maybe we should get some practice in before we go and get buck wild tonight."

"You don't have to ask me twice," he said as he picked me up and marched down the hall towards the bedroom before tossing me onto the bed. There was a wicked gleam in his eye that made me so hot, and an idea popped into my head as I stripped off my sweater and jeans. Something that would show him how much his decision meant to me.

"Jackson," I murmured to get his attention as he whipped off his shirt. I was distracted by the sight of his chest for a moment before I realized he was standing there, staring at me. "I want to make tonight as special for you as you made it for me, but I didn't have time to plan something in advance."

"Any night I get to spend with you is special, sweetheart," he reassured me.

"But tonight's different. Things are changing, moving to the next level. Your decision to move with me to New York? It's huge, Jackson. You're making sure my dreams come true just the way I imagined them," I tried to explain.

"That's the idea, Kaylie."

"Then I think the least I can do is try to make one of your sexual fantasies come true, don't you think?" I asked.

His pants dropped down his legs, and he just froze there staring at me with a shocked look on his face while they lay tangled at his feet. "Any one of them in particular or did you have something specific in mind?"

I gave him a seductive smile as I lay back on the pillows, lifting my arms above my head. I crossed my wrists and rested them on the headboard before saying, "What do you think?"

"Kaylie," he breathed out, staring at me spread across the bed clad only in my bra and panties. No other words were said before he moved into action.

He kicked off his jeans and swiftly walked into the bathroom. I heard him slamming some cabinets as he went in search of something to tie me up with. At least that's what I assumed he was searching for. I heard a ripping sound right before he came back in the room with strips of a torn sheet gripped in his hands.

"Are you sure about this? You don't have to do this to pay me back for my decision. I made it for me as much as I did you."

"I want this, Jackson. I've been curious about it ever since our first night together. I was scared before, but I'm ready now. You've proven to me that I can trust you with anything," I reassured him.

"You can trust me, sweetheart. I swear to you, I will never do anything you aren't comfortable with. If you don't like it, you just tell me to stop," he promised.

I just smiled at him and held my hands out to him. Now wasn't the time for words. It was the time to show him I was ready for this.

He pulled off my bra before looping one of the torn pieces of sheet around my wrist, tying it loosely before wrapping it around the bedpost. His fingers trailed down my arm and across my chest, pausing so he could tease my nipples before he moved to do the same to my other wrist. He gently nudged me so that I moved down the bed a little, laid bare and vulnerable beneath him. Sitting on his knees, he looked down at me, one fingertip running lightly across my skin, sending goose bumps everywhere it touched.

He leaned down to whisper hotly in my ear. "I swear to God, I'm going to make this good for you, sweetheart."

"I have no doubt about that, Jackson."

His slipped his fingers into the sides of my panties as he tugged them down my body. Once they were off, he held my ankle as he moved one of my legs to the side as he looped another piece of sheet around it so he could tie it to the bedpost at the foot of the bed. He ran his palm up the inside of that leg, lifting it slightly so that he barely touched my pussy as he crossed to the other side to run it down that leg on his way to secure it to the other post. I had expected to be uncomfortable lying naked and spread out before him with no way to move or cover myself. But it wasn't uncomfortable at all. Instead, I felt powerful, which was a very strange thing considering I'd put myself at his mercy for now.

His eyes flared passionately as he looked at my body. "Fuck, Kaylie. You have no idea how beautiful you look like this. It's even better than I imagined when I pictured it in my mind. Are you comfortable?"

I shook my head at him. "No, Jackson. I'm not."

He gave me a concerned look. "What's wrong, sweetheart? Is it too tight?" he asked worriedly.

"Not too tight. Too slow. Please, I need you now. Don't make me wait," I pleaded.

A relieved expression crossed his face before he flashed me his smug smirk. "Naughty girl. I should make you wait after scaring me like that. I could, too, and there wouldn't be anything you could do about it, would there?"

He didn't really expect an answer to that question, but I still found myself shaking my head in response. His cocky attitude was turning me on so much. He always enjoyed himself in bed with me, but he seemed really playful right now. And it was making me so wet. I wiggled my hips a little, testing to see how much I could move. It was just enough that I could lift my body off the bed slightly.

"Does my Kaylie need me to touch her?" he murmured as he reached out to stroke the inside of my legs with the palms of his hands. If they hadn't been tied up right now, I swear I would have tightened my legs on him so they'd be trapped. I really did need him to touch me, and I looked up at him pleadingly.

He must have seen the desperation in my gaze because he

swiftly moved into action, stroking and touching me everywhere he could reach. He paid particular attention to my breasts, knowing full well how much he could turn me on by playing with them. He cupped them in his hands and squeezed gently before pushing them closer together so he could easily move between my nipples, flicking them with his tongue and sucking them into his mouth. The puckered tips were practically begging for more as he switched his attention back and forth between them, the cold air hardening them further each time his mouth abandoned one. I didn't think he left an inch of my skin untouched by the time he'd worked his way down my body before he finally turned his attention to my drenched pussy. By this point, I was desperate to come.

"Oh, God," I whispered, incredibly turned on by the whole experience. I'd had no idea I'd love the feeling of being under his control so much or I would have agreed to try this much sooner.

"Let's see how many times I can get you to say that tonight," he teased before kissing down my stomach. He stopped to swirl his tongue at my belly button while his hands wrapped around my inside thighs, resting right at the seam where they met my body. I knew he could feel how incredibly wet I was for him when his grin flashed triumphantly across his face. "I bet I can get one out of you right now, couldn't I?" he asked as his thumbs inched towards each other. He slid the tips of both thumbs just inside me, teasing me by not moving fully inside. I tried to move, but I couldn't go far enough to drive them any deeper.

"Please," I whimpered.

"Please what, Kaylie? You need more?"

"Yes," I hissed out.

"I don't think you do," he said before wrapping his lips

around my clit and sucking it into his mouth.

The pressure combined with the feel of him swirling his thumbs at my entrance was enough to set me off.

"One," he murmured before licking down my slit to ram his tongue inside me, his thumbs holding me open for his probing tongue. He fucked me with his tongue so deep that I could feel his chin digging into my ass.

He was relentless, holding me in place even though I couldn't move. My feeling of helplessness just heightened the experience, and before I knew it, I was climaxing again. He didn't stop licking me, and I was so sensitive at this point that I could barely take it anymore.

"Jackson, no more," I begged.

"Two," he replied.

"Fuck me now, Jackson. Give me number three with your cock hard and deep inside of me. I feel so empty," I whispered, pulling out the big guns to turn the tables a little in order to get what I wanted. His eyes flared even hotter at my words. I knew how much he loved when I talked dirty to him.

He stood up to drag his boxers off his body, his cock springing free from its confinement. He ran his hand down the shaft as he looked at me on the bed before grabbing a condom from the bedside table. I loved watching him touch himself, but I needed him inside me now, so I was thrilled to see him roll it down and climb between my open legs.

"You ready, sweetheart?" he whispered in my ear, his cock resting at my entrance.

"Now," I whimpered.

It was all the encouragement he needed. He pulled his hips back and slid deep inside with one smooth stroke.

"Fuck," he groaned deeply.

"Hard and fast, Jackson," I pleaded. Now wasn't the time for anything else.

I felt his hands lift me up as he placed a pillow under my lower back, tilting me up and changing my position slightly. I felt him slide even farther inside, deeper than he'd ever been. He slowly moved backwards, his cock dragging out of my body. I thought for sure he was going to tease me like this all night, but as soon as he left my body, he slammed back inside as deep as he could go. Then he tortured me again by slowly pulling out. He kept that same rhythm for a while, alternating between slow exits and hard thrusts until I reached the point where I started to tighten around him as I neared another climax.

"Now, Kaylie. Give me number three and I will give it to you hard and fast," he commanded.

It was enough to push me over the edge again, and he picked up his pace and started to hammer me into the bed. His hips pumped back and forth over and over again as fucked me harder and deeper than ever before. I wanted to hold on to him, but I couldn't even get any words out as my climax went on and on, feeling like it would never end. Waves of pleasure kept rolling over my body as his cock bottomed out each time he drove inside. It felt like he was growing harder with each thrust, and I needed to take him with me.

"That's right baby. Fuck me as hard as you can, Jackson," I whispered to him. "I'm all yours. You can take me anyway you want."

My words spurred him on even further, and he leaned down to capture my mouth in a hard kiss as he thrust one final time before I felt his cock throbbing deep inside me as he came.

****

"I can't believe that you're really going to come with me, Jackson," I whispered after I recovered from having my mind blown by what we'd just done in bed. It had taken a few minutes to catch my breath and get the blood flowing again after Jackson untied me. I was still stunned by how far Jackson was willing to go to make our relationship work. But so very happy.

He tilted his head down so he could gaze directly into my eyes, our lips almost touching. "Of course I'm going with you, Kaylie. I don't think you understand exactly how much you mean to me." He pulled my hand up so that it rested on his heart. "You have owned me from the very start. This heart? It beats for you, sweetheart."

My pulse raced at his words as I melted inside. I knew Jackson cared about me, but this was something else entirely. Ours might have been a whirlwind romance, but that didn't make the feelings between us any less real.

"I love you," I blurted out, unable to keep my feelings bottled up inside. The words might not have been as pretty as the ones he'd just given me, but they sure seemed to do the trick. His eyes lit up and he tightened his hold on me.

"Thank fuck," he uttered, "because I love you, too. Just in case you didn't get that that's what I was trying to say."

I pulled back a little so he could see how serious I was about my next words. "I think I've known for a while, but yeah, I definitely understood what you were trying to say just now. It was probably the sweetest thing anyone has ever said to me in my life. Best moment ever."

He flashed me his cocky grin, the one that drove girls wild. "No, Kaylie. Best moment until now. Because I'm going to spend my days trying to top that from now on. This is just the beginning for us. We've got our best days yet to come, sweetheart."

ACKNOWLEDGMENTS

My boys – Thank you for not complaining too much about the piles of laundry & carry-out meals while I was writing. I love you!

Mickey – I am so grateful to have found an editor like you! Thanks for putting your mad editing skills to good use for me. This book seriously wouldn't have released on time if you weren't so amazing!

Kari – Thanks for another crazy hot cover.

Yolanda – You've always been there for me, and your friendship means the world to me. Thanks for being my number one cheerleader!

Crystal, Midian & Harper – Thank you for your insight & offering up some of your precious reading time to help me out.

Love Between The Sheets Promotions – Thanks for your help getting the word out about my books. Natalie has been great and you all have done an amazing job pimping me! The bloggers that work with you have been so generous with their time and efforts on my behalf.

Indie Romance Author Chicks – I have no idea how I got so lucky to have met you all, but I thank my lucky stars that I did!

ABOUT THE AUTHOR

I absolutely adore reading - always have and always will. My friends growing up used to tease me when I would trail after them, trying to read and walk at the same time. If I have downtime, odds are you will find me reading or writing.

I am the mother of two wonderful sons who have inspired me to chase my dream of being an author. I want them to learn from me that you can live your dream as long as you are willing to work for it.

When I told my mom that my new year's resolution was to self-publish a book in 2013, she pretty much told me "About time!"

Connect with me online!

Facebook: http://www.facebook.com/rochellepaigeauthor

Facebook with Indie Romance Author Chicks: http://www.facebook.com/indieromanceauthorchicks

Twitter: @rochellepaige1

Twitter with Indie Romance Author Chicks: @RomanceChicks

Goodreads: https://www.goodreads.com/author/show/7328358.Rochelle_Paige

Website: http://www.rochellepaige.com

SOUTHERN SEDUCTION BOX SET HOLD YOUR HORSES

Charlotte thought she was doing the right thing when she decided to go away to college. When graduation comes and she needs to decide if it's time to go back home and settle down, she worries that she's not ready yet.

Shane has waited four long years for Charlotte, after agreeing to a long-distance relationship because it was the only way to keep her in his life. He can hardly wait for her to come home so they can finally start their life together.

What happens when the girl who is nervous about settling down to small-town life comes home to the guy who is ready to pop the question? Will Shane be able to convince Charlotte that their wait is over and now's the time for them to move forward? Or will Charlotte decide to end their relationship so she can move on to greener pastures?

OTHER BOOKS YOU MIGHT ENJOY

UNTIL NOVEMBER

By Aurora Rose Reynolds

November is looking forward to getting to know her father and the safety of a small town. After leaving the Big Apple and her bad memories for Tennessee, November starts working for her dad at his strip club doing the books. The one time she's allowed there during club hours she runs into Asher Mayson. He's perfect until he opens his mouth and makes assumptions. November wants nothing to do with Asher but too bad for November, fate has other plans.

Asher Mayson has never had a problem getting a woman, that is *until November*. Now all he can think about is making November his and keeping her safe.

Warning 18+ sexual content and a strong Alpha Male.

AXEL

By Harper Sloan

Prologue

God… please let him be late. Traffic? Boss needed help? Hell, at this point I would even pray for his shoe being untied.

ANYTHING to give me just five extra minutes.

Taking a frustrated breath, I remember… I gave up pleading to the heavens years ago. Ten years to be exact. The day *he* walked out of my life. The day the sun stopped shining and my world turned gray. The day that my dreams turned into nightmares. I miss my dreams, the sun, and I miss *him*. So fucking much, even though I know I shouldn't. After all, what good does it do to miss a ghost?

Come on… come on…. I silently beg the light to change. Why is it that the only time I'm running late, every single light catches me? "Fuck! Just fucking change!" I just know if I am not home in the next ten minutes all hell will break loose. *Finally*, as soon as the light turns green I slam on the gas. All I need to do is hurry and everything will be fine.

Right?

I roll into the driveway at 5:45, throw the car in park and rush into the house. Thankfully I had enough foresight when I left earlier to start the slow cooker. "Okay, Okay…" I mutter to myself, while rushing around the kitchen island to the table. If I didn't hurry… nope, I can't go there. *There* would cause me to lock up in fear, and cutting it this close, I can't lock up.

"Deep breath, Iz… just breathe." I remind myself, setting the bowls of chili down. As quickly as I can manage I set the table, make sure the glasses are spot free and the silverware is perfectly aligned. I was *not* going to make those mistakes again. Rushing back to the kitchen, I make sure I've washed and dried all the cookware, and signs of my slow cooker use. I have just enough time to make sure that my 'face', as he so lovingly calls it, doesn't look like I just rushed my duties.

At 6:05, on the dot, I hear the garage door rolling up. *Breathe.* A few moments later, he walks in. Of course, he would never be running late. God forbid he would make it home a minute past his normal scheduled time. The world might end, sky might fall, and pigs might start flying.

No, not my husband; he is never off his game.

"Good evening, Isabelle. How was your day?" He asks, while unloading his arms of his coat, briefcase, and keys. He makes sure his coat is hung perfectly; wrinkles wouldn't dare mess with him. Even they know not to poke the bear. After he disposes of his cell, wallet, and other pocket shit, he finally looks up at me with his cold, dead eyes.

Permission to speak has silently been granted.

"Good evening, Brandon. Things were normal as always today. Did some laundry, ran the errands you asked me to do, and got home around three. I know you said your parents are thinking of coming this weekend, so I wanted to make sure I had enough time to get the spare room situated before I started dinner."

Lies, all lies … just enough to hopefully make him think I wasn't out.

"Hmmm," he states, while rolling his sleeves up. "So," he looks up with his evil smirk and those dead eyes. "That wasn't you I just saw speeding down Oak Street like the bats of hell were on your bumper, Isabelle?"

Fuck. Me.

"Brandon, I swear it's not what you think." I squeak out. Shit, this is going to be bad. "Dee stopped by, she's in town and just wanted to say hi, catch up a little. I haven't seen her in six months- -"

His smile stops me cold, immediately I start backing away. *Oh shit, I know that look.*

"Now, now… Isabelle. What have I told you about Denise? Hmm? If I remember correctly, it was something along the lines of you are not to talk, call or take calls from her, and you are definitely not to FUCKING SEE HER!"

He's starting to step closer now. Frantically I look around for an escape, but he's blocking my only exit. "You have been told, and I would have thought you learned this lesson six months ago. Isn't that how long you said it's been? What do I need to do for you to get it through your dumb fucking head? Jesus Christ, you're a stupid fucking bitch." His eyes are so cold as he steps right into my space. "What part of you being mine, and only mine, did you not understand the last time I was forced to explain this to you. I will not share you with fucking anyone. Do you hear me, Isabelle?" He sneers my name like its very presence on his tongue disgusts him. I've hit panic mode now, he has me backed into the wall, no escape in sight. "No fucking person in this goddamn world is allowed you. Only. Fucking. Me!" He continues, his eyes bugging out and his spit hitting me in the face. "You're nothing but a stupid fucking slut! Isn't that right, Isabelle? I should have walked the other way that night at Fire. I should have known a bar slut from a mile away. But, no! It's all your fault my dick wouldn't walk the other way." He rears back and slaps me hard across my cheek. I squeeze my hands into fists, digging my nails into my palms to keep from screaming out. I can feel the blood running down my neck from the cut his ring must have caused on my jaw. I might be stuck, but I'll be damned if I will let him break me.

"What did I fucking say, Isabelle? NO DENISE! No afternoons chatting like little fucking bitches. You're to be here, cleaning my fucking house, cooking my fucking dinner, and spreading your fat fucking thighs for my dick!" He reaches out and grabs a bowl of chili, throwing it with all his strength against the wall. I watch chunks of meat, beans and sauce run down my happy yellow walls. "And what in the fuck is this shit? I told you, you fucking bitch, I wanted lasagna. Does that look like lasagna?" I should have seen it coming, but my attention was still focused on my happy yellow walls and the globs of dinner still rolling down. I was just turning back to him when his fist hit my temple, momentarily making my vision blur. At least that seems to have knocked some sense into my sluggish brain. I dart to the right, quickly trying to escape the second fist I know will soon be following. Too late, always too late, I catch the second one in the ribs, knocking the breath right out of my lungs. Brandon grabs my thick hair and with a twist of his wrist, I'm right back at his mercy.

Mercy I know he doesn't have.

Throwing me into the hallway, with what feels like the strength of ten men, he's quick to follow with a kick to my stomach. "You stupid bitch. You just can't listen. I own you, all of you. No one else. No one else touches what is MINE. Especially not fucking DENISE! I warned you what would happen. No, I promised your dumb ass what would happen if you went near her again." Kick… slap… punch… kick. "You're never going to learn are you?" He's panting with exertion and it's taking everything I have not to let the blackness overcome me. Even if I know numbness would be following quickly.

I lost track of how long he stood over me, screaming and beating, alternating between his feet and his fist.

Freedom, that's all I crave now.

I close my eyes and pass out.

~~*

When I wake up, the house is dark. Every bone, muscle, and hair on my head hurt. I can't take a deep breath without wanting to die. I can feel wetness on various parts of my head and body. *Fuck*. It's never been this bad. I can't hear anything out of my left ear, what the hell happened to my ear? Fuck, I need to move. Clutching my arm around my middle, I slowly climb to my feet. I take a look around, out of my very swollen eyes, and see that dinner is still sitting on the table. The broken bowl, chili dried to the wall, and even the spotless cups are sitting there mocking me. With a slow and silent step I glance into the living room. No sign of Brandon. Shuffling, more like dragging myself to the kitchen, I see his keys are gone. Holy shit! He's not here. Never, not once in six years has he left me alone in the house after a 'lesson'.

I walk along the wall, holding on for support until I reach my purse, unzipping the side zipper; I reach in and take out my phone. The phone Brandon doesn't know I have. I'm not allowed to have a phone, and he disconnects the house phone and takes it with him when he leaves. I can barely see enough to turn the phone on. I slide my finger across the screen and unlock it. Finally, after a few wrong buttons, I place the call.

"Hello? Hello, Iz? Iz, are you there? Is everything okay? IZ??" I can hear her, she's practically screaming. But I can't get the words out. She knows I wouldn't be calling this late. Hell, she knows I wouldn't call at all.

I take a shallow breath, and rasp out the only word I need to bring my salvation.

"Help..."

Then the blackness pulls me under.

Chapter 1

(Izzy)

I haven't always been this weak person… this broken woman. I used to dream, and when I did, I dreamt big. I had plans, plans of a future so bright it would blind you. I can still remember the day those dreams, those grand plans, and that future as bright as the sun went poof.

I just didn't know it at the time.

At the time I thought everything would be okay. After all, what seventeen-year-old girl doesn't think she's invincible?

That, coincidently, was the same day I decided fate hated me. No, she didn't hate me… she loathed me. People say karma is a bitch, but I have news for you, karma doesn't have anything on fate when she is after blood. Not a single thing.

I wish I knew what it was that set fate on the path of my doom. Maybe it was just being born? I like to think I was at least okay there. My parents loved me, they prayed for me, and I was everything to them. So, no, I don't think that was the day.

Or it could have been the day I stole Maggie Jones' pudding cup. But Maggie was a bully, never nice and always stuffing her face, so I like to think I did her a favor.

I once stole a chocolate bar from the grocery store, but seriously? Fate would have been after every little teenage shit if that was the case. Point fingers all you want, but where I come from it's like a rite of passage.

No, I think fate decided she hated me the day I walked into Dale High School freshman year and my path collided with Axel's. It would make sense that the reason she hated me was the reason for all my pain.

The reason I'm convinced fate will never shine in my favor again. Why would she? She took it all away. Wiped out every single thing I had ever loved in one swift kick.

One day I might figure it out, the reason fate hated me, Isabelle West. But, until that day I damn sure will be careful with my dreams and my plans; my heart and my soul.

Fate might hate me, but that doesn't stop me from hoping one day she forgets about her favorite chew toy. When that day comes, I hope karma has some fun with that bitch, fate.

Made in the USA
Charleston, SC
22 March 2014